W9-CMA-883

NOV -- 2001

Lazarus, Arise

Also by Nicholas Kilmer

Poetry (Verse Translation)
Poems of Pierre de Ronsard
Francis Petrarch: Songs and Sonnets from Laura's Lifetime
Dante's Comedy: The Inferno

Fiction (Art Mystery)
Harmony in Flesh and Black
Man With a Squirrel
Dirty Linen
Lazarus, Arise

Art (Biography/Art History)
Thomas Buford Meteyard
Frederick Carl Frieseke: The Evolution of an American Impressionist
Travel Memoir
A Place in Normandy

Lazarus, Arise

DISCARD

Nicholas Kilmer

Poisoned Pen Press

CHANDLER PUBLIC LIBRARY
22 S. DELAWARE
CHANDLER AZ 85225

Copyright © 2001 by Nicholas Kilmer

First Edition 2001

10 9 8 7 6 5 4 3 2 1

Library of Congress Catalog Card Number: 2001090167

ISBN: 1-890208-80-9 Hardcover
ISBN: 1-890208-90-6 Trade Paperback

All rights reserved. No part of this publication may be reproduced, stored in, or introduced into a retrieval system, or transmitted in any form, or by any means (electronic, mechanical, photocopying, recording, or otherwise) without the prior written permission of both the copyright owner and the publisher of this book.

Poisoned Pen Press
6962 E. First Ave. Ste. 103
Scottsdale, AZ 85251
www.poisonedpenpress.com
info@poisonedpenpress.com

Printed in the United States of America

*For
Jacob
Maizie
Sarah
Christopher*

Chapter 1

The old man dropped. His arms jerking out sideways made his things fly up and away from him in conflicting spirals. Fred grabbed the rolled newspaper out of the air at the same time as he reached to hold people back. "Man down," he called, "give him room…" and looked for blood. Shrieks developing among them alerted the travelers. They began to press against each other in two directions—forward to enjoy, and backward to recoil from, the fallen man. Fred knelt over him. The old fellow was breathing, but he'd gone the same green-gray as the linoleum floor of Logan airport's terminal E.

The crowd, swelling forward as the plane emptied, began to split into new streams, aiming for the other booths in which the officers started to scramble back of their glass, reaching for phones or calling to each other about the activity in the no-man's land between the arrival bay for flight 147 from Paris and passport control.

"Medic," Fred shouted toward the uniforms. He loosened the man's stained brown necktie and opened his shirt. Green as he was, there was no blood outside him so he'd not been shot. He'd looked it, the way his arms whirled out. The bones of his face jutted blue under his pallor. His eyes rolled with his shallow gasps. He needed a shave. Was it alcohol on his breath, or only mortality? Their fellow passengers, filing past, kicked the man's possessions into a heap at his feet. His scuffed shoes were a thin yellowish leather that could be dog. There was a cardboard-looking briefcase. A blue canvas container the size of a gym bag might have been used to transport chickens. The contents of a white plastic sack had scattered: receipts, a black eye mask, lozenges, and four little bottles of the red wine they had served on the plane.

"Get medical help fast," Fred told the first uniform to appear above him, that of a very pink man with short red hair who dithered without bending. "Tell them heart, or stroke: something like that," Fred said.

"Move along folks," the officer shouted into the crowd. "Nothing to see here. Please move on."

It was another three minutes before Fred was joined by enough uniforms to assure the sick man room. Nothing yet in the way of medics—but one agent moved into the stream of arriving passengers asking for medical volunteers.

"No, I don't know him," Fred answered a question. "Just happened to be behind him." Once enough uniforms had collected they'd rolled the man onto his side and two of them held him steady, one propping his head on her thigh. The sick man wore a dark brown corduroy suit that had seen better days. His cloth cap had come off, exposing a mottled head, mostly bald, but with unkempt straggles of gray hair back of the ears. "You'll take it from here then," Fred said, standing and shouldering his bag again, before he turned for the nearest booth.

"Pleasure," he told the agent, responding to the question glanced across half-glasses, when the officer wanted to know what Fred had been doing in Paris on a four-day trip. He hadn't been able to buy Clayton Reed what he'd gone for, since Clay at the last moment had come over chintzy, refusing to allow a bid of more than a hundred grand for a Sargent watercolor any fool would know was worth the quarter million it had sold for. A bid as feeble as Clayton's hardly qualified as business. Pleasure didn't cover it either. The trip had proved to be an elaborate extension of Clayton's native ambivalence. Much as he loved the painting, he despised Sargent more.

He'd had no luggage to check through, but the emergency had held Fred up. By the time he got to customs the baggage area was crowded with loaded trolleys. However, the customs agents had gotten wind of the potential for pedestrian snarl that was back out of sight, where the planes emptied. They'd been given the word to move things along. Customs barely gave Fred a nod as he passed beyond their influence and into a lobby packed with its afternoon gaggle of family greetings, punctuated with the odd driver carrying a sign reading C.O.P.A.C. or MR. PERKINS. Among them was someone waiting for a skinny old man in a brown suit—father, uncle or grandpa—who was in for a sad surprise over the loud speakers? "Would the person meeting Mr. X, repeat, Mr. X, please report to the…" and so on; however they did it here.

Only as he pushed through the doors and reached the sidewalk did a couple of medics appear, carrying tools of their trade and moving at a pace calculated to allay anxiety in the public. "He's in a bad way," Fred reminded their backsides.

While he waited for the shuttle bus, the lime-green Massport fire and rescue trucks started pulling up to the curb, upsetting the stream of taxis. And an ambulance siren, at some distance, added color.

⁓

This had been a slow, damp, golden autumn. None of its effect could be appreciated until Fred got out of the subway at Charles Street station and started on foot for Clayton's place on Mountjoy. Beacon Hill was bathed in a glow of brick and gold, warmed by an afternoon sun that had not yet slanted into evening. All the antique- and coffee- and what-not-shops were open for the Friday trade that ought to keynote a strong weekend. Fred swung through the pedestrians, eager to stretch out after the plane's cramped quarters.

The air was sweet and vaguely sad, tainted with the somnolent decay of the year's turning.

"You return empty-handed," Clayton Reed complained, descending the spiral staircase into Fred's work space, which occupied the ground floor of Clay's town house. Fred had dropped his bag and shed his old blue blazer, and was looking through the debris on his desk. Clay, dressed in a tan linen suit, looked as if he were headed for a wedding, his usual condition. The thick strands of his long white hair were teased into a tousle. He plucked at it while he addressed Fred with a petulant inquiry that the lean features of his face subverted into the appearance of mere good manners.

Fred answered, "True, I was not in a position to bring home the Sargent. However I did pick up a newspaper against which you may test your French. It is the *Canard Enchaîné.*" Fred retrieved the rolled paper from the wastebasket into which he'd dropped it when he discovered the thing under his arm as he put down his bag. The newspaper had held its shape on account of two red rubber bands, one at each end.

"Today's," Clay approved, accepting the token. "We shall see what these jokers have to say concerning Jospin's blunder. It will make a change from Thomas Pynchon, who is simply unfathomable. Nothing satisfies after Proust. I regret my decision to grapple with Pynchon. I suspect sometimes he means almost to be funny! Never mind. I leave you, Fred, to recover from your journey. Is there anything I need to know? Anything out of the ordinary brewing in Paris?"

Clay glanced around Fred's study as he chattered, taking in the clutter of books, periodicals, and paintings propped where they could be considered. At principal issue these days was a small Church landscape whose central cow had a moose in its ancestry. Clayton had taken it from a New York dealer on approval, but with no intention of buying it. He owned a better one. He just wanted to gloat, then send it back along with a catalog of its defects.

"Strikes on the subway lines," Fred reported. "Randolph bought the Sargent, naturally, with Bloom and Mirko both sitting on their hands in the front row, at Drouot Montaigne. So they knocked it out between them afterwards, or much as those three pirates hate each other, if none of them can control it for himself, they'll own and sell it together."

Clay slapped the paper on Fred's desk, causing a flutter among the mail and reference materials. After this outpouring of impatience, calm claimed him once again. "You may be fatigued," he offered.

Fred nodded, sitting at his desk and hooking the phone toward him.

"I weary of elegant ladies," Clay explained, smacking the newspaper against his thigh. This must be his tardy rationale for refusing Fred a decent bid on a good picture: a triple portrait of Sargent's nieces in a landscape composed of wind and flowers. "And nothing else caught your eye in all of Paris?" Clayton yearned. Because it did happen sometimes that Fred picked up a picture on his own, without consulting Clayton, if it was intriguing enough as well as cheap.

Clay waited until he was sure Fred was not going suddenly to recall that he had purchased an unexpected Chase or Botticelli, before he sighed and said, "I shall not need you before Tuesday." He started up the stairs again, waving the newspaper in farewell. "And I do thank you for this. Most thoughtful, Fred."

Fred waited until the cordovan shoes had vanished into the ceiling before dialing Molly's number in Arlington. He put his feet on the desk and leaned back when he heard it connect. At the fourth ring it clicked onto the recorded treble voice of Sam, Molly's son, striving for depth. "You have the right to remain silent. You have the right to get a lawyer. You have the right to, oh, I forget the rest of it. Leave your message. Everything you say *can* and *will* be used against you." Then Sam's rare laughter, followed by the beep.

"I'm safe back and it's four-thirty," Fred started. "I'm at Clayton's. My car's here, but it's rush hour now, so…"

"Fred," came Terry's voice in frantic interruption. "Leave me alone, Sam! It's Fred. Help Mom with the bags. Fred, what did you bring me?"

"A present from Paris," Fred said.

"What is it?"

"I won't tell you."

"Then what did you bring Sam?"

"I won't tell you."

"Then what did you bring Mom?"

The sounds of rattling grocery bags swept the phone from Terry's voice, and gave Fred Molly's. "Back safe?" she asked. "Sam warned me there are lots of women in Paris."

"The best one sat next to me on the plane coming back," Fred said. "Fascinating creature. She talked the whole trip. Italian. It didn't bother her that my Italian is on the weak side. She…"

"You sure you want to keep on about this woman?" Molly asked.

Fred went on, "She reminded me of your sister Ophelia. Not only because she's blonde—hers is natural—but the way she expects to be waited on…"

"Were you thinking of spending the night in Arlington?" Molly asked. "Or do you have a subsequent engagement?"

"My fellow passenger?" Fred asked. "Oh, I don't know. She may be too much even for me. Not only did I have to read to her, she even wanted me to cut her meat."

"What?" Molly exclaimed.

"She's three years old," Fred said. "She told me forty-seven times. I'm exhausted. I was giving her mom a rest."

"Fred!" came Clay's shriek of exasperation from the top of the stairs. "For God's sake, man, what is this? A joke?"

Chapter 2

Clay almost clattered down the stairs, trembling with rage or worry or delight. He resembled a tethered pennant in high wind.

"Hold on a minute, Molly. Clay, what's the problem?"

"When you are free," Clay said, noticing that Fred was occupied, "will you come up?"

Fred waved a hand and Clayton retreated. "What's all that?" Molly asked. "I haven't heard Clay so upset since that Christmas party when I tried to interest him in Ophelia."

Fred said, "I'll have to find out. I'll be in Arlington as soon as I can."

"And you can tell me all about your blonde. No, Sam. Put it in the freezer. No. Not before dinner. Don't argue with me. Yes, Fred?"

"Let me see what's eating Clay. Then I'll hit the road."

Clay's agitation, as he paced in the first floor room he called his parlor, was acute. Fred could hardly take in the current display of paintings from the collection. Clay had brought the Fitz Hugh Lane out of storage, and had it hung so that its subject, the schooner *Hester Prynne*, sailed through Boston Harbor back of the grand piano.

"It is unlike you to indulge in such a prank," Clay scolded. "Suppose I had inadvertently damaged it?"

"Fill me in," Fred demanded.

"Do not prolong this. What is it you brought me? It is simply beautiful. I am bowled over."

"Pretend I am in the dark, and show me," Fred suggested.

"I can't believe…" Clay stared at him with the alert suspicion of the paranoid, before he led the way across a wilderness swamp of oriental rug, dodging side tables, until they came to the grand piano on whose Kashmir shawl the newspaper was laid open. On it a large page sparkled with color. One side, the right, bore two columns of script, interrupted by frequent small illuminations. But it was the left side that took the eye, and the breath, and held them. There, in a green summer field, peasants were making hay with scythes, indifferent to the group commotion in the foreground. A man, reclining in a tomb, his grave clothes all disheveled, gazed up at what must be Jesus. Around them men, averting their heads, busied themselves with the raised lid of the sarcophagus. The women held their noses.

"*Iam foetet*," Clay read, pointing toward the script beneath the painting. "'By now he is stinking. It's been four days.' A rough translation, Fred."

"It's John eleven," Fred confirmed. "The raising of Lazarus. You don't mean to say that thing was rolled up in the paper?"

"It comes as a surprise?" Clay tested, his demand electric with suspicion. "You are not toying with me? How, then, did you come by this?"

"Jeekers," Fred said. "I reckon I stole it."

"That's not like you," Clay disapproved. "Although it is magnificent. And the *Hell*, on the opposite side, the verso, is perhaps even more arresting. Forgive me. Why did you steal it?"

"Sheer inadvertence," Fred confessed. "Sorry, Clay. I'll have to give it back."

Once Fred had explained, Clayton went into mourning which was quickly followed by the swervings of enlightened self-interest. "The man was smuggling it out of France," Clay concluded. "An illuminated parchment of this quality—it must be early fifteenth century! The watchdogs of the musées nationaux would never permit such a treasure to leave French soil! Did anyone see you with it?"

"I'll have to find that man," Fred said. He and Clay continued to stand in front of the parchment, captivated by the purity of its color, the fine detail, bits of gilding; the masterful assurance, also, of the scribe's hand laying the story out in words for any who could not read the picture.

"Yes, but suppose *he* was stealing it?" Clayton objected. "Let me prepare you a drink. We'll consider the implications. As you have often heard me say, no one can ever truly own a work of art. We are but transitory curators."

"Meaning, 'Can we keep it, hunh? Since it followed us home?'"

Clay stroked the side of his nose and turned away, asking, "Sherry?"

"I'll see what you have cold in the fridge," Fred countered. "But first, as long as we're here…" He took the large skin gently by the corners of its left margin, lifted it, and turned it to the other side, exposing for an instant the leering face of Jospin, caught by the *Canard*'s photographer. The vellum was light, thin, and creamy; supple after all these years, as if the animal from which it came had only yesterday been as lively as were the paintings. Hell glared from the second side; a dark well-organized cataclysm of damned souls and naked functionaries over whom Lucifer, reclining on a grill, presided shamelessly. The composition was of knots and spirals, with touches of gold and vermilion pricking against the gloom. It was, to link their contexts, the awful fate from which Jesus, on the other side, had rescued Lazarus. This side, like the other, was embellished with ornamental borders and complex initials, the text laid out in both red and rich dark color that might either be called black or brown.

Each page represented weeks of brilliant labor. It was far too much to take in so quickly.

"Whoa, Nellie!" Fred exclaimed. "Clay, this is serious." He slid the sheet of parchment to one side, removing it from the newspaper's inks and acids, and letting it rest on the Kashmir shawl. "You can read the script?" he asked. "I always think I'm getting a word or two of the Latin, and then everything runs together."

Clay crossed the room, a glass of sherry in one hand and a small black book in the other. "Once again you surprise me, Fred," he remarked. "How did you know the text was from the gospel of John? You are correct. It is chapter eleven, verse twenty-one—'Martha therefore said to Jesus: Lord, if thou hadst been here, my brother had not died....Jesus said to her: I am the resurrection and the life,' and so on. 'Jesus cometh to the sepulchre. Now it was a cave; and a stone was laid over it. Jesus said: take away the stone...he cried with a loud voice: Lazarus, come forth. And presently he that had been dead came forth, bound feet and hands with winding bands; and his face was bound about with a napkin.'"

Clay looked up from the book and continued, "If this parchment is news to you, as you claim, how did you know the reference to John's gospel?"

"What do you think we did in Sunday school in Iowa," Fred asked, "besides learn to whistle 'Onward Christian Soldiers?'"

Clay flipped pages, took a sip from his glass, said, "Humor me," and read again. "'For nation shall rise against nation, and kingdom against kingdom, and there shall be pestilences, and famines, and earthquakes in places. Then shall they deliver you up to be afflicted, and shall put you to death: and you shall be hated by all nations.'"

"'And then shall many betray one another,'" Fred picked up. "'And shall hate one another. And many false prophets shall rise, and shall seduce many. And because iniquity hath abounded, the charity of many shall grow cold.' Matthew twenty-four. I won a blue ribbon and a baseball hat." He marched into the kitchen whistling "Onward, Christian Soldiers."

Coming back with a glass of soda water, he found Clay standing at a safe distance from the piano so as not to drip sherry onto the parchment. The air between him and the painted skin was frank with lust. Fred looked at his watch and growled, "They're not going to tell me a blamed thing over the phone, even if I find someone to talk to. I'll drive back to the airport and ask questions."

"Hear me out, Fred," Clay pleaded. "I have been thinking. Suppose we have made a major discovery? The man you describe, carrying such an object, concealed, was up to no good. Without your quick action, it might have been lost forever. I tremble to think...but it is safe now. Let's think on the appropriate next step."

"It rubs me the wrong way to steal from a man when he's down," Fred said.

"From what you say, he won't be looking for the—I suppose we must call it a manuscript—today," Clay objected. "He, or—what about this?—his contact. His underground, black-market contact. What about that? Who was the man meeting? An officer from Sotheby's? A double agent? There could be repercussions." He placed the ends of his long fingers on the edge of the parchment and stroked it with the tentative intimacy a teen-ager might try upon another teen-ager.

"Then again, once I find him," Fred said, "there's other questions also, like what else was the man carrying?"

Clay shivered like someone who notices a tornado frisking on the horizon. "If we become visible," he objected, "by asking questions—suppose we drop what's in our grasp in order to reach for something we cannot see? Many a loss has come about through greed."

"We have nothing to lose," Fred argued. "The parchment is not ours. Not yours. Not mine."

"Tut, Fred. Naturally I shall recompense the rightful owner, once I am satisfied that said rightful owner has been found. I do not assume the rightful owner to be the man you have described." Clay's eyes flickered involuntarily across his perfect clothing. "I am uneasy. Fate has given us temporary control of what may be a significant treasure. In prudence, before we act recklessly, let us learn what it is. Lest we abet a crime…the man was smuggling at the very least…it is a risk but with your permission, risk though it be, why not consult with…? I shall confirm my selection with Ben Marlowe. Ben knows this field and I do not. My instinct is that we might do well to consider this with Hannah Bruckmann."

Chapter 3

Hannah Bruckmann turned on the stoop, dismissed her taxi with a wave, and handed Fred her briefcase.

"Fifty thousand dollars in books," she remarked. "Go easy with it. I make the driver watch me until I get inside. On Beacon Hill, you never know."

Somewhere in her middle or late forties, she was dressed in brown slacks and a poncho affair that had been woven on purpose in that shape in South Asia. She could be called small only if one compared her to someone else—and she did not invite comparison.

Clay, standing behind Fred in the doorway, made room for her to enter. She passed through the entrance hall without a glance at the walls, or rugs, or furniture; simply followed Clayton impatiently into his parlor as if she were oriental royalty compelled, by a lamed camel, to seek overnight shelter in Versailles. She acknowledged Clay's gesture and sat on the edge of a love seat.

"Based on your telephone message," she started, "you believe you have something?"

The bluntness of her opening made Clay twitch. He faced her, sitting on the sofa over which hung the Copley painting she ignored, the portrait of a young man holding a squirrel captive on a golden chain. "Judging from your excitement, and also because I respect our mutual friend Ben Marlowe, I closed early. Normally on a Friday evening I keep my doors open until eight o'clock."

"May I offer refreshment?" Clay demurred.

"There is no refreshment that does not damage books," Hannah Bruckmann replied. "Even the passage of time. Mine is limited. And frequently expensive."

While Clay considered his approach, Fred had wandered toward the doorway to the kitchen, in case she wanted a drink. They'd agreed to let Clay handle this, since although the project was Fred's baby, their contact, Ben Marlowe, was a friend of Clayton's. The book dealer carried no purse; only the briefcase, which she'd left with Fred. Her hands perched ready on her thighs.

Clay began, "Ms. Bruckmann, you are used to situations that are confidential and anomalous." Hannah Bruckmann raised her eyes without bothering to speak. "Benjamin Marlowe speaks highly of your expertise and your discretion. Also," Clay coughed, "he mentioned that you are an extraordinarily capable business woman."

"If you have something to sell and I buy it, I am prepared to pay what it is worth," Hannah Bruckmann said. "If I must. If I own something you want to buy, you will pay what I think it is worth, regardless of what I paid. Ben tells me you are eccentric, nobody's fool, and honest but not candid. 'If you get him to admit anything,' Ben said, 'it's true, but it's not the whole story.' Now we know where we are. What do you have to show me?"

"The matter is delicate," Clay began.

Hannah Bruckmann nodded. "You want the gift not only of my expertise, but of my silence."

Clay hastily amended, "You may bill me for your time."

"I will, unless there's a purchase to be made. Is that the situation?"

Clay shook his head, stood, and led the way to the piano. He'd covered the parchment with a pillow case so as to hide it while he sized up Hannah Bruckmann. When he uncovered it, the book dealer's face remained impassive.

The parchment lay with the *Lazarus* miniature up, as Fred had first seen it. Because the approaching dusk muted the light from the bow window overlooking Mountjoy Street, Fred had put a lamp next to the subject. Hannah Bruckmann took a small magnifying glass from the pocket of her poncho and began to study the parchment, her attention completely absorbed. Her hair swung forward as she studied; dark and straight, and cut simply at the base of the neck. Even in the earlier conversation her face had remained placid. She worked five minutes, only looking, saying nothing, touching nothing, before she glanced at Clayton and asked him, "I may turn it over?"

"Certainly."

"*Hell.*" She nodded when she saw the dismal crowd scene, and she muttered, reading part of the text beneath it.

"It's St. John's gospel," Fred said. "The raising of Lazarus, obviously, on the first side."

Without responding, Hannah Bruckmann continued to study the page, then turned it over again, withdrew a retractable tape from the same pocket that had produced the glass, and began to measure. "Four hundred ten millimeters height," she exclaimed, shaking her head. "That's sixteen inches. The margins have never been cut. Almost unheard of. And the width is five hundred eighty—almost twenty-three inches; over eleven inches per page." She spun and glared accusingly at Clayton. "Sam Fogg has seen this folio?" she demanded.

"Who is Sam Fogg?" Clay asked.

"Meaning that my question is out of line," Hannah Bruckmann acknowledged. She held the parchment up to the light and stared through it, examining the opacity of the letters; the inks and paints and gildings of the borders, initials and filigree designs; the faint marks where the scribe had ruled the pages prior to laying out the text: minuscule openings, pinpricks, where the light shone through. Then she laid the parchment down, covered it with the pillowcase again, and crossed the room to sit on the love seat she had adopted. "I'll take beer," she announced. "Is this what you have, or is it a sample?"

"Pretend we are as ignorant as we say," Fred suggested. "I'll get your beer. When I get back can you approach the matter as if I'm a bright eighth grader who got lucky at a yard sale?"

When Fred returned from the kitchen with bottles and glasses for himself and Hannah Bruckmann—Clayton would stay with sherry—Clay was trying to show off. "Because," Clay was explaining, "since I am able to follow the Latin, there's what appears to be an incoherence, a backward break in the text, where the scribe, under the miniature of Lazarus, tells that story; and suddenly he switches on the right hand side to John baptizing in the Jordan river. The sentence having to do with Lazarus doesn't even finish. Did you notice that, Fred, in the initial on the right hand side—beautifully executed—next to the painting of Lazarus? John baptizing within the letter O, under a golden tree? Curious juxtaposition. The Jordan river opposite the tomb. Very suggestive."

"This will take time," the book dealer said. She accepted a beer, poured and tasted. "You know something about paintings?"

Clay smirked an affirmative.

"In that case you realize that there is always the possibility of fraud. So few of us do not want to demonstrate how smart we are. When we add our intelligences to the trickster's trap, often we do his work, becoming his accomplices. We convince ourselves by bringing to bear our own superior knowledge. I say *his* work, since few women are forgers. We women write optimistic checks, yes—but we seldom have time or patience for executing the long con."

She took a deliberative drink while Fred got comfortable, watching Clay squirm. "You declare this a forgery?" Clay demanded. "After ten minutes?"

"Having said which," Hannah continued, as if Clay had not spoken, "it is very hard to forge the object I have just examined. Its chemistry will need to be tested, in addition to the study of its style and its iconography. Please take notes on what I say. I hate to repeat myself.

"My first response is: this is an exceptionally large and beautiful folio, probably from an illuminated book of gospels, made in the first decade or so of the fourteen hundreds. The script is Gothic. The pages are ruled in both red and plummet. The drawing of the miniatures is masterful. I see no signs of later overpainting. It's not Italian. The Italians romanced the contrast between flesh and hair sides, accentuating the roughness of the hair side. I say French, presumably Paris, because the vellum is so smoothly prepared that without greater magnification I can't judge which is the hair side and which the flesh. The vellum is so smooth on both sides, in fact, that—this is unusual—the artist or artists (I believe I see more than one hand) were able to paint miniatures on both sides of the folio, whereas normally only the flesh side would be used. The skin is probably calf. It could also be lamb or kid. Some scholars pretend they can distinguish. I don't think they can.

"As literate persons you think you know books. Many who live in houses think they know houses: but not how they are built. What you showed me is a folio, one sheet, which was originally folded in the center. Unless it's perfect-bound, a strictly modern development, a book in the Western tradition is still normally made up of gatherings, or quires, usually of four sheets at a time, placed one inside another, and folded, like newspaper pages. Then each gathering is sewn together down the center of the fold, as well as to the perpendicular support—a cord or strip of vellum—that keeps the sheets together as well as holding them to the binding, what you call the cover. Binding is a different art from printing. Even today it's seldom the same workshop that does both. Caxton was an exception. Of course your folio was made before Gutenberg but, give-or-take the printing press, the process of making books hasn't changed much in over a thousand years.

"You are confused about the order of the text, Mr. Reed, because your folio is actually four pages. If it's one of a gathering of four sheets—keep it simple, suppose it's the first gathering in the book; the first sixteen pages—the outside folio has to comprise pages one, two, fifteen and sixteen. If that side is upward, you find page one on the right hand side, and sixteen on the left, facing each other, as on the opposite side pages two on the left and fifteen on the right would face each other. You follow? I mean if you take it out of its gathering, as has been done in this case, and look at it by itself. Then the second sheet in is pages three, four, thirteen and fourteen. The third is five, six, eleven and twelve; and the last, seven, eight, nine, ten—but not in that order because even here you'd find page ten on the left of the fold line, and seven apparently following it, on the right.

"They had all kinds of tricks to get the folios and gatherings together properly, because the person buying a 'book' bought the written or printed sheets, then carried them to the binder and started haggling for the kind of cover he wanted. And then most of the old books got taken apart and put together a dozen times over the years. When this happened like as not the pages were cut down. Maybe the owner wanted to use a jazzy binding he saw, that was too small for the page size, or the binder wanted parchment trimmings to boil down for glue. You expect a big book, such as this one was, to get smaller over time."

Hannah Bruckmann took a deep breath, looked Clay in the eye, and said, "This isn't what you want to know. I'm stalling because I'm interested and suspicious. Some things don't figure. For example, in the *Lazarus*: that symbolism, death and harvest—though it could be inadvertent—it's almost a hundred years before its time. You'd expect it in the Renaissance. Think, for example, of Ronsard's '*Si le grain de forment ne se pourrist en terre.*'" She waited without success for Clay to acknowledge his failure to recognize what she was quoting.

"The folio is beautiful, yes," she continued. "But I want it to be beautiful, so I may not see it correctly. I'm not comfortable. I've seen that tomb before. It's all too familiar."

She stood, leaving most of her beer, and said, "I'll telephone you tomorrow. Maybe the next day. Or Monday. Your folio is interesting. Unless it is a fraud, it is valuable."

Chapter 4

"She can barely contain herself, she's so excited," Clay proclaimed after seeing Hannah Bruckmann out. "You saw that poker face?" He stopped, noticing that Fred was on the phone.

"No, nothing on the local evening news," Molly was saying. "Which only means he's not an interesting person. Why do you ask?"

Fred said, "I picked up something the man dropped, not noticing, what with everything going on. It is of value to him. I'm going back to the airport. If I'm going to find out who he is, I'll have to start there. Don't know when I'll get to your place."

He hung up and turned to silence, before they started, Clayton's passionate objections. "It is the decent thing to do," Fred said, shrugging. "I'll leave the folio where it is until I know more. It's safer here." He took the *Canard Enchaîné* from the piano and began looking through it minutely, page by page, searching without success for anything more than the printed word. "You still have those two red rubber bands?" Fred asked.

Clay located them on his left wrist, where he had slipped them in case of future need. Fred put them as they had been at either end of the rolled newspaper. "Given its contents, in case someone was on the lookout for that paper, I may as well fit that much of the profile," he said.

Clayton warned, "Suppose this was, or is, a criminal affair?"

"Not unlikely," Fred agreed. "I'll keep in touch—unless you plan to go out?"

"I must have first refusal," Clay insisted. "Make sure you get me that. It is only fair. It is I who saved the folio from certain oblivion. Fred, that was no act? You had thrown it away, had you not?"

"Can't say I hadn't," Fred acknowledged.

"Then you must acknowledge that I have a moral claim."

"I have a hard time, as you know, admitting the concepts *moral* and *claim* into the same sentence," Fred said. "It is a difference between us. Beyond coincidence you have no claim at all. You like it and you want it. That I understand."

"Regardless, and not in any way wishing to impede your honorable purpose," Clay said, "do get me the right of first refusal, will you? And, before you go, Hannah Bruckmann. What's your first instinct? Do you trust her?"

"Of course not. No more than I trust Ben Marlowe."

———

The snarling end-of-the-week traffic working its way from Boston's downtown toward the airport tunnel gave Fred time to think. He stared out the window of his car at the rich yellows of the willows and ash trees along the river. Even the maples had chosen gold ochre as their autumn color this year. While he stared he objected, "What are we talking, several thousand bucks?

"Since he was on a Paris flight, we know the guy was in Paris this morning long enough to get the plane. If he was in transit, where was he coming from? Bulgaria? Saudi Arabia? There's got to be tons of things like this ready to come out of the old Iron Curtain countries; or the former Soviet Union states…"

Shortly after eight o'clock Fred found a place for his car in short term parking and, leaving his bag locked in the trunk, took an empty stool along the bar that offered itself to stranded travelers or family members awaiting delayed flights in the lobby of terminal E. He had let the paper show, swinging it as he entered the building, and he laid it on the bar next to him when he sat.

One person was tending bar, a woman in white dress shirt and black pants. Their little oasis was crammed in next to a coffee stand and a place where, if it were open for business, sushi could be had. Fred ordered beer and told the woman, "That was some commotion earlier."

"It's always something," she agreed. "Beck's all right? Or you want Miller's?"

"Miller's on ice. How did it turn out? Was someone here to meet him? See, I was on the same flight. I got to wondering."

"You mean the ambulance and stretchers and all that?" she asked. "You still here? That was hours ago."

Fred agreed, "Goddamned delays and cancellations. It's always something, isn't it?"

"That's what I always say," the bartender said, shaking her head. "It's always something. And if it isn't that, it's something else." She turned away to flourish a rag along the counter.

Fred persisted, "Stretcher, you said? They took him out past you, through customs? Through the lobby? How'd he look?"

"Like he'd taken his last airplane ride, frankly," the bartender said. "They had him wrapped up all the way, you know how they do, with the blankets strapped around him. Head and all. From the talk I knew it was a him. Anybody here to meet that party, they wouldn't know to recognize him unless they were expecting King Tut."

"Airplane food," said a man in a blue suit, and in an advanced state of decomposition, seated on Fred's right. "Five dollars says six jokes on Ledderman tonight about airplane food. You going far?"

Fred said, "What do you recommend?"

"Anything but Omaha."

Shortly afterwards Fred put the question to a security guard, "Any information coming through yet on the dead guy from that Paris flight?"

"Check with the public information office if you want, but they will tell you zip. Who you with?"

"I'm independent."

"You want to show me something?"

Fred promised, "I'll make sure you're not quoted."

Molly Riley had risen to the top rank of monsterhood. Although it was Friday evening she was making her children do their homework. They were seated resentfully at the kitchen table. Molly had come around the house and met Fred when she heard his car clatter into the driveway. She'd taken off her reference librarian outfit and slid into weekend garb: blue jeans and a black flannel shirt that had once belonged to King Kong. The dark curls she wore short had a few glints of gold in them from a big willow behind the house that had begun to shed.

"Find something to eat and join me in the yard," Molly had ordered. "And don't give the kids any sympathy. I'm tired of having my Sundays ruined. There's meatloaf, which the kids didn't eat because they sneaked a sub after school. They made a deal if they had to do their homework early I'd give them their allowance early. Get what you want. I'm drinking really bad red wine."

"Mom hates us," Terry told Fred, looking up angrily from her *Words are Magic* workbook. "What did you bring me from Paris, Fred?"

"Oh, shut up, Terry," Sam urged from across the table. Pencil in hand he was seated in front of a sheet of lined white paper on which he had written the title, "Whats In My Room."

"When you finish your homework, come out back and I'll give you your presents," Fred said. He started rummaging for food.

"She gives us these boring things to write that according to her the great writers of the past already wrote. Like anyone in the world cares what's in my room except Terry because I won't let her in there."

"I go in all the time," Terry said. "It's boring."

"Is your teacher going to check to see if what you write is true?" Fred asked. "Will she look in your room to see?"

"I'll kill her if she even tries. Like she can't even get in the door without that thing, a subpoena. Could she?"

"How about you have something in there she hates?" Fred asked. He cut slabs of meatloaf and pulled bread from the fridge. "Thanks for leaving me all this food. I'm out back when you're finished."

"Did you see the Eiffel tower?" Terry asked.

"See it? Heck, I jumped off it. But not from the very top."

Molly's back yard abutted five others. The houses in the neighborhood were small. A good deal of sky stretched around and over them, big trees reaching into it, scraping their leaves in response to the light wind of evening. Spy Pond was not far away. Molly, seated in an aluminum folding chair, was reading the morning's paper with the aid of the light cast from the kitchen window. A canopy of gulls and crows crossed the sky, fighting, heading in the direction of the nearest water.

Fred shifted another chair until it was more or less on level ground. He was too large for it unless it was balanced just right. "The honest truth is I brought you chocolates that I hid under your pillow. When you find them I want you to be surprised."

Molly looked up from her paper. "So the Paris trip was a bust?" she confirmed.

"A bust with maybe a problem in its tail," Fred agreed. "I have to get some sleep before I can work on it. The man died. That's all I could find out at the airport. Not even his name. I told you on the phone what he had with him. I can't return it until I know who to and, to be on the safe side now, since I'm involved, what it is. And I have to keep Clayton honest also, since he shows signs of espousing the fortunes of war theory. That or he wants to horn in on this occasion to outdo that…who was the guy in the classics so honest they couldn't trust him? Threw him out of office?"

"Aristides the Just." Molly went back to her paper. A few leaves shuddered down from the Ousemans' willow at the foot of the yard, across the fence. The wind took them on a slant that carried them left, toward the Proctors' yard. Fred had a bite of his sandwich, chewed and swallowed, and washed it down with tea. "You appear subdued," Fred said.

"I am." Molly continued to read the paper.

"The kids? Something at work? Your mother? Me?"

"Sometimes it does seem like an awful load of kids. Sorry, Fred. Welcome back from Paree. Thanks for the chocolate. I'll be surprised. If you didn't bring anything for Terry, you have to go back."

Fred pulled the box from his pocket and opened it to show Molly. "It's a silvered charm of the Eiffel tower. I put it on a chain so she can hang it around her neck. For Sam I have telephone cards. It's the big thing now. They do a roaring trade in used ones at stalls behind the Grand Palais—from all over the world. They're decorated with all kinds of parrots, snakes, temples and monuments. People trade them like baseball cards. What do you think? Will the kids like their presents?"

"You have a fifty-fifty chance," Molly said. "You're falling asleep. Sit with me for half an hour, then sack out. If you want I'll get on the phone after and see what I can learn about the man who died."

Chapter 5

When Molly's furtive weight tipped the mattress, Fred asked, "What time is it?"

Molly was still in the black flannel shirt but she'd taken off everything else. Her feet were cold, and rough from a summer of wearing sandals. "Nothing formal or for the record," Molly reported, "pending notification of next of kin. What he died of they don't say. Your man's name was Jacob Geist."

"Good work, Molly. I'm surprised you got even that."

"Friend of a friend of a friend of Dee," Molly said. "Oh, look! What's this under the pillow? Chocolate?"

Fred sat up. "Jacob Geist. That name rings a bell."

"Maybe. There's no address in his passport, but it's U.S. at least. That narrows it down, though he could be a U.S. citizen living abroad. They're going to work through the State Department, which either they aren't going to bother doing until tomorrow, or the State Department's computers are down, or nothing happens during the weekend, or I don't know whatall. Don't wake up. There's nothing you can do."

Molly's teeth exposed the soft green center of a chocolate. "Pistachio," she approved. "Unless it's marzipan. It could be three or four days before they get to the autopsy, according to the friend of a friend of a friend of Dee, because everything's backed up anyway, and the weekend is starting where even coroners have to golf and pick apples with their families. And besides they like to get the green light from the next of kin before they start dismembering the person, you know, unless there's something…sorry. You want a chocolate?"

"Not exactly," Fred said.

"Will you settle for a chocolate?"

"Only with great reluctance."

"How reluctant can you get?"

"Not being a man of many words, I'll show you," Fred offered.

———

When he woke in the dark he was saying, "It's got to be. *That* Jacob Geist." He was mercilessly awake. The dull glow on the clock's face, next to Molly's, told him it was three a.m. He slipped out of the bed and made for Molly's bathroom in order to stand under her shower.

"Who are you talking to?" Molly grumped as he slunk into the bedroom again.

"Jacob Geist. Unless it's a different Jacob Geist. If I ever knew, I don't recall what he looked like. It's been a long time since his *Line of Sweetness*. He's—the man in the airport—the right age. I'd often wondered what became of Jacob Geist."

"And now you know. He died. What's the *Line of Sweetness*? Then let me go back to sleep."

"It can wait."

"Maybe it can. I can't. You've got me curious. I won't sleep unless I'm satisfied."

Fred sat on the edge of the bed. "Subversive landscape artist he called himself. This was way back, in 1976, when Smithson and Christo and that gang were not old news. Good thing for Jacob Geist Nixon was having so much trouble." Fred chuckled. "The *Line of Sweetness* was as subversive as you could want a work of art to be. Unamerican, the boys in suits called it. Nixon would have stopped it if he could, but by that time other people were busy stopping Mr. Nixon.

"No one knew it was coming until it was there. On July 4, 1976, the country's bicentennial, Geist's *Line of Sweetness* appeared as if by magic. At dawn on Independence Day folks began to discover it on the ground, first in small segments—sticky patches across highways, that disappeared into the grass. Then people noticed how the trail swept on across houses, parking lots, woods and shopping malls. Reports of the appearances of fragments of the line became so numerous, over so many hundreds of miles, that the police and air force—people didn't know what the substance was. It was dark and sticky and some thought it was blood, or excrement—took to helicopters to discover Geist's *Line of Sweetness*. It was an irregular border of molasses about six inches wide, attended by crowds—of people, animals, and insects, many of them butterflies—starting on the Atlantic coast, at the corner where New Jersey, Delaware and Maryland meet Pennsylvania, then extending westward along Pennsylvania's southern border until it picked up the Ohio river bank and continued, following the old Missouri Compromise, 36 degrees thirty minutes west of the Mississippi. Geist had redrawn the Mason Dixon line.

"It was never learned how Geist put it together. His guerilla organization worked so efficiently that many concluded the work must have been done by Communists from outer space, the same ones who brought us Roswell and the lines at Nazca, and the Mars canals."

"Go on," Molly demanded, rolling over and closing her eyes. "I can still hear you," she said, pulling Fred's pillow over her head.

"The authorities displayed outrage," Fred went on. "In a democracy, outrage is what authority believes it is elected to achieve. They tried to nail Geist for trespass by means of molasses. Some senators, angry at having their ceremonies in Philadelphia overshadowed by this circus trick, tried to find and retroactively to suppress Federal funding at work, but they failed. Rain washed the molasses away and they couldn't even get Geist on willful destruction of property. They had nothing left to complain about except that this former citizen of what was now East Germany had chosen the occasion of our bicentennial to remind us of the still oozing wound of slavery, sweet with rot; and of its continuing infection in the culture of discrimination."

Molly snored.

"It was brilliant. Then, after 1976, if you can believe it," Fred finished, "I never heard another word about Jacob Geist. Not—if it's him—until now."

He lay on top of the bed until he concluded that sleep was out of the question. Then he dressed, slipped down to the kitchen, and fried himself some breakfast.

Molly's kitchen remained dim, since Fred lit only the bulb over the stove. His eggs and meatloaf spat while he put bread into the toaster and started water for coffee. If she could get away with it, Molly wouldn't light the furnace until Thanksgiving. The house was chilly, friendly, though somewhat mournful with its proper occupants asleep. Fred, the odd man out, operating in a limbo of lost time, sat at the table with his meal and pushed Sam's composition, *Whats In My Room*, far enough away to keep it safe from ketchup. "Alot of times my snakes get loose," Sam had begun, "and crawl where I can't count them."

"Fight terror with terror," Fred said. "Good boy, Sam. If my Jacob Geist is that Jacob Geist, what was he doing skulking into Boston with that parchment?"

Fred conjured up the folio again and looked at it more carefully, in memory, now that he was alone. The fragment was eloquent of a time and culture almost entirely remote from today's Arlington, Massachusetts. This was true in spite of the fact that the pictures could be followed, and the language could be understood as little by Fred now as it had been then by whoever had ordered the book it had come from. Still undiscovered by Europe's militant piety, Arlington, at the time the manuscript was being made, was a fecund wilderness of sticks and fish and game and weather untouched by cities; its few indigenous people had a couple of centuries still to enjoy the notion that their version of civilization was the last word in the concept.

Once the twentieth century had run its course, although one could pretend to have inherited many of the ideas assumed by the maker of the manuscript, the world was utterly changed. The civilization from which the miniatures had come was dominated by a military-ecclesiastical complex of interlocking families who maintained a cruel if chaotic order in spite of the wars, famines and pestilences that rocked the European middle ages—most of which were their own doing.

Whoever painted that *Hell* knew firsthand the pecking orders of court and bureaucracy. Those devils bustling around the lounging top cock, Satan, were so naked as to seem in uniform. Smoke spiraling upward from hell's fire was peopled with the descending souls of the common damned, while from either side of the foreground a demon entered dragging, by the neck, a more illustrious catch. These souls were dressed, or you would not know their importance. One was a bishop, complete with crosier and miter. The other, from the richness of his clothing, was of the nobility also: *also*, since in those days bishops came only from noble families.

The acts of torture and manhandling represented in this composition were observed, not merely invented. In the same way the haymows in the placid landscape behind Lazarus had been recorded by someone who had looked out of his window and watched the harvest being made.

"Unless it's a fraud," Fred reminded himself. "Which is what Hannah Bruckmann wants us to fear. But leaving room for errors that arise from self-delusion, the thing feels genuine to me.

"What became of Geist? Has his work been a factor in the marketplace? If so I'll find him that way—but not at four in the morning Atlantic time."

Fred went outside to stand in the chill dark of Molly's back yard. Though within easy commute of Boston, Arlington had managed to hold on to its distinct identity as a town rather than melting into the generic wasteland of suburban sprawl. The slow night wind carried the scent, and the damp, of Spy Pond, whose natives tasted so strongly of its mud that Sam, who fished them out relentlessly, refused to eat them. Molly had even tried dousing them in curry, but still the mud prevailed.

Fred itched to be at work, or to go fishing, or to be moving in some real direction. He left the yard and sauntered through the quiet streets until he came to the pond. It lay out flat and black in its many acres of muddy water. His access point was a grassy playground that became a beach where, during the hot months, children swam while their parents or nannies gossiped or napped under the trees. Sam and Terry often stopped by here after school, with friends, to play a pickup game of ball or just to hang around the jungle gym and talk. The teen-aged kids normally wouldn't appear before dusk when they'd indulge in solitary fishing, group basketball, or the conversations that develop around bottles of Colt 45 Malt Liquor passed in paper bags.

Many small boats lay upended in the grass where they'd remain untouched until spring brought warm weather again.

Here in the darkness, with no one else visibly alive, the illusion was that Fred stood in the center of expanding circles of peace. They moved out across the darkness gracefully, as if all civilization were not, in and of itself, utterly dependent upon human cruelty.

Chapter 6

Walking more or less into the dawn, Fred took his time working along the six or more miles from Arlington to Boston. He had nothing useful to do. The time and the exercise gave him room to think, or even better, not to think. It was morning in America. Big trucks were out, blowing black smoke while they delivered strawberries from Mexico.

Fred stopped for coffee at the Boston end of Longfellow Bridge and carried it with him to Mountjoy Street. He let himself quietly into his office, deactivating the alarms he had persuaded Clay Reed to install even though Clayton refused to acknowledge that art and monetary value ever found a tangent in reality. Art and money, he insisted, are entities as different from one another as language and begonias "which do not refer to one another as begonias, mark my words, Fred," Clay insisted.

But Fred had found an argument which began, "It's also true that the value of your life is hard to measure in begonias. However, if a burglar with a club believes that your life stands between him and an object he thinks of in terms of how many fixes it converts to in the currency of heroin..."

From the shelves in his office he pulled out last summer's *Art in America* index.

"Well, lookie here," Fred crowed after flipping back and forth between relevant pages. "Geist got himself hooked up with Armand Kordero. Just last year Kordero was showing something he calls *Geistmaps*. So Jacob Geist hit the big time in New York."

There'd be no one to telephone at Kordero's before ten o'clock. Fred lay on the old leather couch and stared at the ceiling for three minutes before he said, "Forget it. I'll walk in and surprise them."

A surge of damp heat had moved in to confuse New York. It did not warm the city since it hung in a belt at knee level as if it were composed of a substance other than air. The haze of autumn gave the city's gray stone and cement an aura of antique gravity. When Fred climbed off the airport bus downtown the bustle of Saturday morning activity had already set in. Fred started walking.

Five years or so earlier Armand Kordero had moved uptown, announcing to the world that Soho no longer had a soul. He'd made his name in the hysterical boom of the eighties, when almost anything called art that could be packaged (not necessarily *framed*) could also be marketed. While others jumped onto the bus of "dead art" as Kordero called it—the impressionists, or certain of the favored old masters: even major works done in the fifties by folks like Jasper Johns or Willem de Kooning, who clung to life—Kordero found and groomed streetwise new kids who had gimmicks. His casting couch was fabled for its policy of non-discrimination. Those he embraced, he got under contract early, and made them fashionable by marketing the hell out of them. No matter that their principal work was transitory—conceptual or performance art, or works involving dye in moving water, or shadows cast by buildings scheduled for implosion—Kordero arranged grants for them of which, as agent, he then took his cut. He kept them on salary and had them produce, as byproducts to their major efforts, drawings and prints and photographs; ephemera; journals—anything that could bear the artists' signatures. And these things, under the terms of the contracts he made with his artists, Kordero owned.

The artists, meanwhile, looked excellent in severe black clothing, photographed well, were often to be seen nude, or close to, in slick publications, were quoted to and by each other in print, were found in compromising positions with each other, or with Kordero's growing claque of collectors; enacted famous highjinks at exclusive parties; and eagerly fell victim to cocaine, liquor, fast living and adulation. They tended to burn out and to die.

In short, Kordero ran his stable of stars as if he were a movie mogul in the nineteen twenties. Captain Broody had been his creature, as had the high-explosive Cleo Klein, who flamed out in the rust-colored satin sheets of the wax magnate who financed her *Sonoran Desert (((Mirage))) Project*. So as to extend the magnate's enjoyment of his prurient guilt, Kordero had allowed him to finance the memorial volume celebrating Cleo Klein's *oeuvre*, which therefore reproduced the seven hundred works on paper which Kordero owned. No more than a dozen of these, each year, would Kordero "release" to the market.

Though he called all this "living" art, in truth once a young artist signed with Kordero, that artist was effectively on death row. Wyzant and Pleeminster both were suicides. Though her beautiful body was never recovered, Murtaugh was last seen running naked, at midnight, toward a beach in East Hampton, her famous ropes of red hair flying—in a December storm.

In his early days the grit and glitter of Soho had suited Kordero. That was a time when money thought of art collecting as a romp of slumming, fraught with psychic or sexual danger, spiced by financial risk. But recently, in keeping with his own maturing, and with the sober middle age his original artists would have reached had they but lived, Kordero had taken a third floor space on 57th Street, in the gauntlet stretch where many other, long-established galleries had hunkered down to weather the market slump. To buy from Kordero now was to "invest" in stocks he had created, which he liked to describe as blue chips.

The art of commerce seldom gave Fred much amusement: commerce in art, never. A Kordero would take and sell, if he could, the cry of passion issuing from a stranger's bedroom; the print of a girl's first menstrual blood; the lampshade made from human skin. Kordero was far from the noblest of the breed of the tribe of art dealers, who were at best merchants of death, all of them, in Fred's opinion. But one could not love the captive without doing commerce of one kind or another with the captor.

Fred pushed the brass-bound revolving doors into the lobby, nodded toward the doorman at the desk, telling him, "Kordero," and took the stairs up. He'd left Molly's house dressed in khakis and the black flannel shirt Molly had, in due course, found cumbersome; so he looked either like someone with no money to spend, or like a rich person who doesn't care what he looks like.

Kordero's occupied the entire third floor, on three sides of the lobby area into which the stairway led. The exhibition spaces inside could be seen through plate glass walls, along which, facing out, hung a selection of large-scale works on paper sparely framed in chrome, or black wooden moldings. Well inside the double glass entry doors behind an empty desk sat the stupefyingly lovely girl they use in all these places, whose natural endowments have given her practice making lightning judgments whom to encourage, and who deserves the immediate cold shoulder.

Before he'd start fooling with the foreplay, Fred began by strolling around the lobby area looking at the works displayed there. Murtaugh was represented by a print made from her own hair, which she had drenched in black ink and then run under the steel roller while she lay naked on the bed of the press. True, the procedure had resulted in an image that conveyed a whirl of interesting worry—well advertised (rather, *documented*) by the enormous color photographs of the process, which hung next to the print. The actual color of her hair showed only at groin and armpits. The print—called, fairly, a monoprint, since it was unique—was exhibited with a label giving its title *Hair # 109*, and its price: $18,000.

Each of the three walls around the lobby was formed of two storefront-sized panels, separated and held by brass hardware. Because one panel was taken up by the entrance doors and posted informational flyers, that left space for displays for five from Kordero's stable. Each panel contained one original image and documentation concerning the artist and the work. In one was an *Unnumbered Yellow Stream # 17* by Manuel Pignatelli. This was an exceedingly simple drawing, in crayon on brown paper, that the gallery described as "absurdist minimalist. $15,000."

Pignatelli's major contributions had been in the field of performance art. His death—documented, like everything else—had come about at the hands of an angry mob that took exception to the performance he was executing at the Taj Mahal. It was, therefore, the final act in a tragic series. Photographs on either side of the drawing showed Pignatelli urinating on the Hele stone at Stonehenge; the altar of the sun at Machu Picchu; St. Peter's; and the Sphinx. The drawing, *Unnumbered Yellow Stream # 17*, was a "preparatory study" for the work at Machu Picchu. (The act at the Taj Mahal, performed *alla prima* in the artist's "mature phase"— he was twenty-seven—had resulted in no drawings.) Though *Unnumbered Yellow Stream # 17* had been drawn with crayon on crappy wrapping paper, it had been signed and dated and titled in ink, in the artist's hand, and was declared to be listed in the *catalog raisonné* of Pignatelli's works.

"Enough," Fred said. He rang the bell and entered when the stupefyingly lovely girl buzzed the door open.

"The thing about you, Fred," Molly had told him once, "when people see you coming they start to remember all the bad things they have done. You can't help it. It's not that you look mean, exactly..."

The stupefyingly lovely girl priced Fred's shoes, pants, and shirt, added the value of his haircut and probable underwear and socks, and came up with less than a good lunch somewhere if you ordered a glass of wine. She lifted her eyebrows.

"I have to spend a hundred thousand dollars on art before noon," Fred said.

The girl's eyebrows had already risen as high as they could. She was obliged to stand in order to get them any higher. "Is there anything special?" she started.

"I'll look around," Fred told her. "Kordero in?"

"Not this morning," the girl said. She was dressed in tailored white linen that gaped between the buttons when she moved around the desk toward him. Her beautiful long legs were bathed in white silk. Aside from that she was pink and blonde all over: the bubbly blonde cheerleaders' mothers kill for. "I don't expect Mr. Kordero before one in the afternoon on a Saturday when he drives in from the country."

Fred said, "You'll help me if there's something I want. That is—are you empowered to make commitments for the gallery? Like to talk price? Never mind. I'll look around. What's in your windows didn't do much for me." He started toward the room that displayed black paint-splotched manhole covers by a new gallery discovery called Ruta; looked impatiently at the first; then called back, "I know. How about Jacob Geist? You have anything by him?"

Chapter 7

"I only just started here," the girl said. "The name Geist doesn't sound familiar. I'll look." She'd already picked up the telephone to initiate a call, and she had to put the receiver down when Fred interrupted.

"*Geistmaps,*" Fred said, walking toward her. "Now I remember. That's how I heard of Kordero's gallery. Take a look in your files."

"No, see, he keeps the keys to the files. Normally I don't need…see, the thing is, he'll be in."

"My problem is time," Fred said. "I may not like what you have, if you have anything."

The girl made a decision and stood, patting down a panel of her dress that was attempting to lose touch with her flank. "Jacob Geist," she said. "I know there's nothing hanging by that name. But if the person you are interested in is one of Mr. Kordero's featured artist group, he'll have a view book and—let's look in the office."

Fred followed her six paces to the door she opened into the inner sanctum where Kordero's aura hovered behind a horizontal sweep of mahogany desk top. Kordero's version of what one New York gallery of Fred's acquaintance used to call the chloroform room was not the *Belle Epoque* bordello waiting room common to those who sell "dead art." Instead it was glass and chrome, with windows overlooking the 57th

Street action, and three framed pictures hanging. Kordero's chair was a Bauhaus swivel that gave him the window as a backdrop, while his clients, gazing upon him, were permitted to sit comfortably, two at a time, in chairs of padded leather.

Back of Kordero's chair were the phone, the fax machine, the computer. Shelves rose halfway up one wall. In their lower shelves books celebrating such gallery darlings as Pignatelli stood out. The top shelf was filled with severe black spring binders, the "view books" whose lettered spines the improbably lovely girl stooped to read. "Murtaugh," she recited. "Broody, Schlichtman, Waters, Cleo Klein—I love her, don't you? So spiritual—Brad Silence, Distress—she mostly was a singer—Ruta…I noticed you were interested in Ruta?"

She handed Fred the *R*U*T*A* view book opened in such a way as to display the first two pages: the photocopy of a newspaper article showing Ruta being arrested. He'd been caught red-handed while removing a sewer cover from the Cross-Bronx Expressway. Ruta was a gnarly, sniveling-looking individual with a cowlick in front, very lovable. Across from this free publicity was a photocopy of Ruta's check paying the fine, as well as his invoice for the purchase of a replacement cover. All this was an essential portion of the work of art. Without the documentation the manhole cover would be little other than a decorated manhole cover.

"But I don't see Jacob Geist," the girl said. "If the gallery was showing that artist—excuse me, there's the phone." She looked doubtfully at Fred's unyielding presence and decided to answer the telephone, its red light blinking back of Kordero's desk. Fred put the life and works of Ruta back where they had come from, and crossed to the black bank of flat files that had been built into the wall facing the book shelves. They rose to a height of five feet. Each four-inch-deep drawer had a chrome handle beneath which was its alphabetical identity. What was left of Jacob Geist was waiting in a similar drawer in a cold room in East Boston.

Fred pulled the G–H handle and commanded, "Bring out your dead," but nothing budged.

The lavish girl looked up from her whispered telephoning, asking, "Sir, would you care to sit down?"

"I'll browse," Fred said. The three framed works that were hanging above the book shelves were similar to each other in the boringly bland tastefulness that is the trap awaiting even the most subversive artists once they find their niche. One was a life-sized drawing of a cinderblock suspended over the aerial view of a city, such that the masonry appeared to threaten urban society. This work's large signature read Megan Mogan. Was this the preliminary study for a violent installation foisted upon Houston or Kansas City? The second was a succession of bloody concentric blobs, as if both a human arm and a leg had been chopped transversely again and again, and the stumps printed against Rives paper with their natural juices. The third..."Maybe I'll wander," Fred decided, "see what else is in the store."

"...Jacob Geist," the girl had whispered into the phone. "Just a minute," she called.

"I'm taking a look in the next room," Fred reassured her. "What is he, on his car phone?" He wandered from the inner sanctum into the reception area, skipped the Ruta room, and tried the next, where a painter who had heard of Wayne Thiebaud, maybe even looked at him, but never understood him, presented a series of images of oversized ice cream cones being offered to parts of humans not normally associated with eating ice cream. The surfaces were waxy, gleaming and garish, as if the paint had been mixed with styling gel. The paintings were six feet square. But their size could not make up for the artist's inability to draw. Though the exhibition was billed as a retrospective, every image was the same, and each sighed a weary elegance that had long since left behind even the memory of humor. This artist was called Acacia Hospice. She had died last year.

The girl's sudden appearance interrupted Fred's contemplation of a two-foot load of Cherry Garcia ice cream on a cone being thrust into what might be an armpit bristling with larger than life-sized hair.

"I'm Mirelle," the girl told him, as if she'd forgotten that fact until this moment. "Mr. Kordero wants to talk to you. While you wait he wants you to have coffee, juice, whatever. I'm Mirelle."

"Then I'll be Fred," Fred said. "What do you have, a button you press to let him know there's a live one?"

Mirelle simpered. "So, Fred, what can I get you? There's a place downstairs they send up."

"I'm fine," Fred said. "Mirelle, have you noticed how many of the artists die young?"

"It's like a tragedy," Mirelle observed. "While you wait...Mr. Kordero says Geist is a landscape artist? Maybe you want to look at Catesby Lowe. What he does, it's for the ecology, which is today's big thing. He stops people in the street who are wearing these expanding watch bands, that you can get on a Rolex or a Timex. They work the same even when they're gold. And he scrapes the dirt out from between the links with a cuticle stick, and collects it; and when he has enough he takes it somewhere—it could be Arizona or Sri Lanka—and places the dirt into the dirt again. It's very spiritual, like a ceremony, when he does it. His show's on the other side of the gallery. Follow me."

"I'll wait in Kordero's office," Fred said. "Unless—how long will it take him to get in from the country?"

"That's him now," Mirelle said.

Turning away from the Acacia Hospice retrospective, Fred looked through the gallery's glass walls into the vestibule where the elevator's brass doors were whisking open for a man in a dark brown suit.

Someone had taken most of Mr. Kordero and combed it up over the back of his head. Only the raw black hair had remained glued down, thrusting forward so as to resemble bangs. The rest of him, giving in to gravity, had tumbled back in a random fashion that took shape only according to what the man's clothing allowed in terms of bulge and drift. You wouldn't call him fat, but there was too much of him, and none of it seemed to attach to bone. Only the face had a defined character; a chiseled handsomeness that was out of place on the body, as if the body had thrown its own head away and stolen another. Kordero bustled across the vestibule like a machine designed to travel across the surface of a swamp. He waved a hand toward Fred and his assistant. Mirelle hurried to open the door for him.

Kordero's eyes, under the black bangs and too much eyebrow, were the blue gray of a rental vehicle. He held a loose pink hand toward Fred and announced, "Armand Kordero."

"Fred," Fred said, taking the hand before it could fall of its own slack weight. It lay in his grasp as if pleading to be put out of its misery.

"Just Fred?" Kordero asked.

"Like the jewelry store. Let's talk about Jacob Geist," Fred said.

"We'll be comfortable in my office," Kordero assured them both. "Mirelle, I want tea. You already ordered for…?" He gestured toward Fred.

"My wants are few," Fred said, leading the way into the inner sanctum and sitting in one of the padded leather chairs. Kordero closed the office door. "Mirelle thought you were in the country," Fred remarked.

"So many people who come in are just passing time," Kordero explained. He eased into his chair and adjusted himself until he fit the view of 57th Street. His eyebrows twitched. His bangs did not. "You ask about Jacob Geist," he said. His teeth gleamed. "Where were you this time last year? We showed his work for a month. Got a good review placed.

Nothing. Nobody came. Beautiful work. Exciting. *Geistmaps.*"
Kordero stroked the gleaming surface of his desk.

"What can you show me?" Fred asked.

Kordero studied the question while he looked Fred over.
"I have nothing for sale," he decided. "Not at this time. The
set's too precious to break up. A year ago I was ready to do it.
Today—I have many other artists of interest, younger and,"
Kordero chuckled ingratiatingly, "cheaper. Good investment
quality, if that is what you are looking to do."

Fred scratched an ear.

Kordero continued, both hands laid frankly on the desk
top, "I came down, intrigued to learn that a new client was—
forgive me, I am premature—a *potential* client, had asked
about Jacob Geist. Geist is an esoteric taste."

"Not so out of the way," Fred replied. "His *Line of Sweetness*: that even made *Life* and *Time*."

Chapter 8

"Describe your collection," Kordero invited, "so I have a better idea of the scope of your taste and interests. It's obvious you have a good eye and an independent streak, both essential qualities in a collector."

"Even if it's not for sale, I'd enjoy seeing Geist's work, or a sample of it," Fred countered. "If it turns out we have business to do together, that'll be time enough to chew the fat. You don't want to invest your time and talent on me and then discover I'm just another jerk."

"Why Geist? Why now?" Kordero asked.

Fred shrugged. "Why pastrami for lunch and not falafel? Because something you can't recall that happened that morning, a smell, or else a rhyming word, put the idea on the back of your tongue ready to become a concept when lunch became an issue."

"To be perfectly frank," Kordero prevaricated, "I have lost touch with Jacob."

"Artistic temperament?" Fred guessed.

"I am used to artistic temperament," Kordero bragged. "I foster it."

Fred said, "I was curious since, between Geist's installation for the bicentennial, and your exhibition of *Geistmaps*, I had not noticed any mention of Jacob Geist."

"For an exhibitionist, he can be quite a recluse," Kordero said.

"Speaking of recluse, you won't show me his work," Fred said, standing.

"Regrettably," Kordero agreed. "In prudence, until I hear from him…. Tell me how to reach you, should my position change. You're in New York just for the day?"

"I live in Charlestown, Massachusetts," Fred told him. He began writing the Chestnut Street address and phone number on the square sheet of Kordero-embossed memo paper the gallery director pushed across the desk. "Pop an image in the mail, I'd appreciate it. Call when things change. If I'm not in, someone takes a message."

"Charlestown," Kordero said. "Don't fire until you see the whites of their eyes." Without rising, he extended the same sad hand.

"Do you know that while the rebels were setting up their defenses on the crest of Bunker Hill that morning, the British were wasting time formally hanging a couple of their own deserters?" Fred asked. "Everyone had to wait for the band."

"Neither side asked my advice," Kordero said.

Fred, opening the door from the office, bumped into Mirelle. She was carrying a paper cup in a napkin. "I don't want it," Kordero told her. "Throw it away. Is there a last name, Fred? In case I call?"

"Fred'll find me," Fred said.

———

"Thought I was being clever," Fred told Molly after he had persuaded Terry to pass the phone along. "All I know is that the dealer, Kordero, has lost touch with Geist. Correction. All I know is that's what Kordero says."

"So you're in New York?" Molly asked.

"I reckon. It's beautiful weather here. What have you got?"

"The same, I guess."

"Then I'll head back."

Fred was standing at an outside booth across the street from where Christie's had been until Christie's espoused the Rockefeller Center aura further downtown. People argued or cuddled or sauntered past him in solitude. Golden leaves fell from a tree Fred could not put a name to. "You sound sort of down," Fred told Molly.

"Fred, you are suddenly two hundred and fifty miles away and on the telephone," Molly replied. "You don't know how I sound."

"See you later then," Fred said. "You want anything from the big apple?"

"I'm taking the kids shopping for sneakers," Molly said, and hung up, saying something else Fred could not catch. She might be talking to Terry, or to the moon. Had Fred made an appointment today to do something with Molly or the kids, which he'd forgotten? Molly could get like this sometimes and it had nothing to do with Fred.

He walked back to the airport buses near Grand Central. Give or take an illuminated manuscript, his trip to New York had been as productive as the Paris venture except that he had slightly more information than if he'd merely called. He had a sense of Kordero; and he knew that Kordero for whatever reason was playing Geist very close to the chest.

"Hold it a moment," Fred said, watching a red light hesitate before changing. "If word of Geist's death reached Armand Kordero last night, or this morning, he'd be a fool not to hold off selling anything he owns until he figures how the man's death will affect the market for his work: his *Geistmaps*, whatever those are. If Kordero knows that Geist is dead he figures I do too; or else why would I turn up the day after? It's too much a coincidence. But then"—the light changed and Fred and his companions crossed—"why did he say nothing about the death? Why did he say—what did he say?— 'I have lost touch with Jacob'? Why? Because he's a liar. But we already knew that. He's an art dealer."

Fred climbed into the idling bus and sat staring out the window. "Hell, you don't 'lose touch' with your artist. The artist doesn't let you. He has to be important to someone, and probably you are it."

All the way to the airport Fred mumbled and worried at himself. He'd been as cautious as and, if anything, even more circumspect than had Kordero. Each had tried to smoke out information from the other, and each had failed—Kordero to the point where he did not know Fred's last name.

"You don't suppose he improves his stock by murdering his people outright," Fred asked himself, "when his intuition tells him the artist's career curve has peaked?"

He had almost an hour to kill before his plane, which he wasted checking the obits in the late papers and talking to the information desk at the New York Public Library. No, Geist hadn't turned up in any of the Whitney's grab bag monkeyshine biennials, nor at *Documenta* in Kassel, nor anywhere else. Nothing more showed than the year-old *New York Times* Friday paragraph reviewing Kordero's exhibition, *Geistmaps*. The reference librarian read it over the phone. When he'd heard it all Fred was richer by adjectives, but not by nouns. The whole review, brief as it was, had been written as if it were intended to serve as the base-line accompaniment to a tune no one bothered to supply: opinion without information.

Though he'd started something moving that might involve Clayton Reed, there was no reason to telephone Mountjoy Street. Clayton was to have driven to New Haven that morning for a two- or three-day sequence of honors and events that was to endow him with a Doctorate in Fine Arts *honoris causa*, as well as an honorary curatorship at the Yale Museum of British Art. These pumpkinifications happened to coincide with Yale's receipt of a large gift Clay had given to the museum. Coincidence? Clayton, given the opportunity in conversation, had responded testily, "Tut, Fred. One does not speak of bribes in academe." He'd bought a new suit for the occasion, which looked exactly like all the other suits he had.

The plane trip provided an unpleasant nap, following which Fred made his way to Charles Street on the subway. Chico's provided him a falafel sandwich, which he dragged to his Mountjoy Street workplace. "Falafel?" he asked himself. "Since when did I eat falafel? What put falafel into my head?"

No argument would persuade Clay to allow answering machine, or even fax, to enter his building. He was convinced these were designed primarily to permit eavesdropping by his rivals. In the past he had been so maddeningly circumspect on the phone that finally Fred, in order to make telephone communication between them possible at all, went through the motions once a week of sweeping the place for bugs that never came. Lacking answering machine and fax, if there had been developments during his absence, Fred would have to go looking for them. He spread his late lunch on its paper on his desk and put in a call to Molly's.

"You have the right to remain silent," came Sam's voice: and so on.

When the telephone rang at five-thirty, Fred, browsing through one of Clay's library's few books that touched on the illuminated manuscripts of the fifteenth century, picked it up expecting Molly's return call.

"Fred, you in trouble?" came the high growl of Rusty Reynolds. Rusty had been at the place in Charlestown long enough to know you didn't put that kind of question to another member of the group.

"Rusty, what's up?" Fred asked.

"Gentleman here looking for Fred. 'Fred who?' I asked him, which he didn't know. So I wasn't familiar with anyone named Fred, and the gentleman obviously didn't get past me."

"He have a name?"

"John Travolta, which you may believe if you want to. You know how sometimes you get that feeling that you get? About this gentleman I got that feeling."

"Interesting. He leave a way to get in touch in case you remember anyone named Fred?"

"He left," Rusty said.

"If he turns up again, I wouldn't mind talking to the guy," Fred told him.

"That'll be hard, unless you're willing for him to get marked some. He struck me as a difficult gentleman to subdue."

"Improvise within reason," Fred said. "Invite him in and give me a call if he shows up again. He's not law is he?"

"Not unless they've improved their cover. He didn't show ID is all I can tell you."

"What does he look like, just so I know," Fred asked.

"Skinny hips, wide shoulders, brown hair down the neck, square face, clean shaven, about forty, huge arms on the gentleman, Northeastern sweatshirt, purple Nike hightops, khaki pants, drives a Ford Taurus wagon, white, old, rusty, with transmission trouble. Full head of hair. Moves like he knows what he's doing and probably enjoys it."

"Carrying?"

"I'd say not. Not this time anyway. Next time, maybe."

Chapter 9

"He's in Charlestown, or was," Molly said when she telephoned after six. "The farces of lore and ordure still don't know, according to Dee's friend's friend's friend, because the address on the passport application is eight years old, when Jacob Geist lived in New York City in a place that has since been torn down in favor of Donald Trump. So the boys in blue are stuck looking down into a big hole in New York. Meanwhile, I found Geist on the Internet, since he gets his supplies from Pearl. You can track anyone down on the Internet, even Thomas Pynchon. You want the address?"

"The kids got their sneakers all right? Why do I care where Thomas Pynchon lives?"

"They're fine for another six months. Not Pynchon. Geist. He's on Arnold Street, more or less next to the Navy Yard. Close to home, wouldn't you say?"

"If you mean close to Chestnut Street. 02129."

"So will you go there, or shall I notify the…"

"I'll take a look," Fred said. "I'm holding something that belongs to someone else; including news of a death—though by now whoever's missing him might have called to ask for accident reports. What number on Arnold Street?"

The bridges connecting Charlestown and its fellow never-never lands to the known world, both the old ones and the newly organized Leonard Zakim Memorial Bridge, rise high and swing from gray steel cables across rail yards, docks, distressed real estate and shallow, dirty water, tempting the unwary traveler from Boston to forget Charlestown and Everett altogether, and maybe try Revere—so long as the traveler can make it alive past Chelsea. The area under the shadow or influence of the bridges and elevated highways is one of those portions of the urban world that is perennially between engagements. The only reason there are not more suicides from them is that desperate folk staring down from them conclude so easily, "That looks worse."

Charlestown is simply blighted by the proximity of the highway and bridge complex. If you want Arnold Street you must skirt the base of Bunker Hill, whose monumental gray obelisk imitates Washington's, then thread your way under the thrumming and peeling highway and bridge supports and past the mixed architectural mistakes of commercial, factory, and residential vacancies overlooking the Charlestown Navy Yard, for whose redevelopment there are often plans under discussion.

Seven Arnold turned out to be a big square building of five floors. Over its front doorway had been carved the date of its conception, 1910, and the words LOVETT SHOES. Below the building's name, in less immodest type, the mason had carved the declaration ENTRANCE above a doorway that had since been filled in with cement blocks. "Charlestown, city of opportunity," Fred said. On the right side of the building was a parking lot protected by ragged eight-foot chain link fence. Behind that sprawled the Navy Yard, as hospitable as the Gobi desert. The factory building to the left of Number Seven was bricked or boarded up completely, whereas only the first two floors of Number Seven were.

"One thing we know about Geist," Fred noticed. "He favored condemned real estate."

Enough was doing even in this part of Charlestown on an early Saturday evening to make this wasteland populated. If no one happened to be walking at this moment along Chelsea or Medford Street, plenty of vehicles passed by. Fred easily found a gap in the fencing around the parking lot and started around the building, keeping next to the wall. The lot hooked around back to where the factory's loading dock overlooked the inlet and the Mystic wharf. Here, next to the double loading doors—closed tight and padlocked—was a second door armed with a call box. Fred tried the GEIST buzzer next to the number 3 and waited for a buzz or click, or a voice through the dirty speaker's grill. Neither of the two other buzzers that bore names—BEAMER on four and KATZ/MONCRIEFF on five—raised a response. A dozen more buzzers went without identities.

"Hell. I'll have to break in," Fred said, giving an irritated shove to the brown steel door—which opened easily inward. A gong clanged and rolled away into darkness, sounding.

"That you, Richard? Lock it behind you," a female voice called from up a flight of stairs just to Fred's left. "I can't come down like I am."

"I'm not Richard," Fred shouted up through her mischievous laughter. "You want me to set up your booby trap again so you know when Richard gets here?"

While he waited for the puzzled silence either to untangle or to dress itself, Fred had a look at the dust and debris of the shabby corridor. Everything, even the ceiling, had once long since been painted the institutional puke green they call "abandon hope." Next to the door the remnants of notices signed "management" ordered tenants to keep the door locked, turn lights off when building not in use, and "no cooking or sleeping in studios. Any infraction will constitute reasonable cause for immediate eviction of such tenant or tenants. Signed, management." These notices were accompanied by a few of the printed or hand-lettered notes and flyers by which artists try to attract the attention of rival artists to their work.

"There's a thing that hooks over the top," the female voice directed. "I hope you weren't startled. Thanks."

"No problem," Fred said. He'd been startled worse. He found the gong and rigged it more or less as it must have been, and took the stairs up, passed the padlocked entrance to the second floor, and pushed through the brown swinging door into the third floor corridor. The female voice had, with a rustling sound, withdrawn higher up the staircase as Fred climbed. She must be Beamer from the fourth floor, with a surprise for Richard; unless she was Katz or Moncrieff from five.

In its glory days the factory's machinery would have been installed on the first two floors. The ceilings on the third were too low for factory space, no more than eight feet. The corridor ran down the center of the building, parallel to Arnold Street. On either side were closed locked doors with nothing other than the vestiges of office numbers on them.

"If he's on the third floor it's got to be one of these," Fred concluded. "And in a place like this, why would I think the buzzer works? Or anything else? What Molly found me is a studio building. The idea is that artists, whom you can treat like shit because they're poor, come into a wreck and make it seem like fun. Then, once it's fun, the owner goes condo, throws the artists out, and cleans up by selling to yuppie couples with two incomes, a small trust fund, and artistic pretensions."

The only light in the corridor came from three low wattage bulbs that hung from the ceiling. Fred studied the corridor. Big freight elevator doors, padlocked closed, lined up above the loading dock, at the end of the building he had entered. He spotted a place in front of one door where the brown-painted pine flooring showed more wear than the rest. The door he faced was steel, and without a name. Fred knocked, not loudly enough for anyone upstairs to hear. After an interval he began working at the door's locks, until he had them open.

He was met first by a haze of golden, dirty light cast from the floor-to-ceiling windows opposite. The light was gold, despite the fact that the early evening sky was broody with a notion of rain. The space he had entered was large, crammed, sifting with dust, and redolent of a persistent, aggressive neglect. Stale cigarette butts, old smoke, and ash were a large part of the smell. Two office wall partitions had been torn out to make a space of maybe thirty by sixty feet. The windows rose the length of the long side, opposite the corridor Fred had entered from. He closed the door behind him, calling out, "Anyone home?" then "Anyone here?" because this was a studio, not a home. Unlikely as it was for anyone to be present, the space was so filled that it would be possible for several people to conceal themselves.

As Fred took in details it became clear that this was, or had been, living space as well as studio. A mattress on the floor, not far from the filthy double sink, had crumpled blankets on it, left as they had been the last time the dead man rose from them. Next to the sink stood a workbench with a hot plate on it; saucepan and frying pan, empty cans and cans waiting to be emptied, and five clear empty vodka bottles. The living arrangements were quickly seen and categorized. The remainder was studio space—and the consequent storage area—of a working artist.

Under the windows Geist had cobbled a long series of drafting tables, using scavenged doors. Of found-lumber and more doors, all painted in different flaking colors as they had been when collected, he had erected floor-to-ceiling shelves along those walls that did not give him windows. All of these were filled, mostly with folders made from found cardboard. Here and there within the room stood islands of odd furniture: a car seat, or a bureau missing a drawer; a bookshelf made of plastic milk crates. It was all quickly seen as Fred followed the waning daylight toward the windows and their bank of tilted drafting tables. Above them, crossing the windows, ran a long shelf, rickety, constructed of many segments. It held pots and jars and cans and boxes and hubcaps full of pencils, brushes, rulers, compasses, paints, and other tools whose uses were not immediately apparent. Stepping through discarded clothing and crumpled paper, Fred reached the last work Geist had been doing.

"That man is serious," Fred said. Along the extended surface what Fred had taken at first glance as printed maps, were intricate original drawings. Serious they were indeed—eloquent and passionate, obsessive not only in their detail but in their originality and technique.

The work was executed on heavy rag paper taken from the many reams stored in the shelves next to the workbench by the sink. That paper had cost money, a level of investment that might seem an odd priority for a man who lived on canned beans and tomatoes.

"No bathroom, Jacob?" Fred asked. "Down the hall, I reckon."

He struggled with the drawings until he realized that they were a sequence, not the same subject more-or-less repeated; that they were oriented with the south side up; that they showed, in high resolution, reading along the entire wall, a portion of the border between China and Tibet. He was finally able to infer this from the couple of place names that showed in one drawing; but it was only because he'd spent some chancy times there that Fred recognized the names of Santangtsung and Polo Gomba. He counted a total of eighteen pictures in progress laid out along the wall, two to each door. Each represented days or weeks of labor just in its execution. The labor of conceiving them would be the lifetime Geist had put in prior to and during their making.

Fred stared in growing pleasure and exhilaration at the unfamiliar human soul laid out before him in such cocky vulnerability. Its presence took precedence over the man's remarkable technique, which Fred began to study. Geist had invented an iconography that fell between the appearance of aerial photography and the cross-hatching used in the engraved steel contour maps of the nineteenth century. A seductive and remarkable intelligence pulsed through these images. To touch one of them was like stroking the skin of a Holbein or a Hockney.

"God, Jacob," Fred exclaimed, stunned. "I'd almost had you pegged as another con artist!"

"Like Michelangelo was not?" snarled Jacob Geist, in the cynical cadence of an old man in his cups.

Chapter 10

For Jacob Geist was in this room: the ghost of him. Fred saw and felt it—felt him—everywhere. The dead man's smell was sour, like chocolate gone rancid. It was this smell that occupied him most while Fred called back his brief but vivid vision of the old man in the airport. Geist stood facing the sink, as if washing his hands, stooped to slightly under six feet. He wore the same brown corduroy suit, its bald and stained places subdued in the studio's dusky light. When he turned toward Fred, color drained back into his face. He had not shaved either today or yesterday, because nobody had reminded him to.

"You think that son of a bitch Michelangelo got the best wall in the world to paint on without knowing how to play the game?" Geist sneered.

"Wouldn't have to, not if he had a son of a bitch like Armand Kordero fronting for him," Fred said.

The dead man wandered vaguely toward him, loosening the brown necktie and removing it to drape it across the back of a tilting rocking chair.

"Might as well, as long as I'm here," Fred said. He followed the old man's ghost to one of the sets of shelves built along the wall opposite the windows. The dust was almost as heavy between the shelves as on the floor and, generally, in the air. From a crackled, blue-painted door waist high, Fred drew a stack of matted drawings, each almost three feet square, and each wrapped in transparent acetate. He carried the pile to the wall where Geist's work tables overlooked the world outside, and not wanting to disturb the present work, spread them on the floor. The old man's ghost stood back, folding its arms and smirking. It moved its lips while Fred read the inscription beneath a flourish of red and yellow ink— a convoluted arabesque: *Preparatory Study. Line of Fat, November 11, 1992.*

"Notice the form of the line. It soars like a butterfly's wing," Geist said.

Fred had begun working down the stack, laying the drawings side by side as he studied them. In the top drawings the line, elaborated in what appeared a repeated free-form, could indeed be seen as the edge of a butterfly's wing, if the butterfly's body were poised, or pinned, on the paper in a horizontal orientation.

"What's the significance of November 11, 1992?" Fred asked.

Geist stood silent as the drawings Fred uncovered became more and more intricate, and commenced to include topography: rivers and hills, roads and rail lines, as well as place names. On most of these drawings the artist had also scrawled, in a crabbed hand, questions, thoughts, and notes to himself, so that, while Fred was studying the meticulous details of Geist's topographical drawings, and registering the content of his working notes, he and the dead man were in effect conversing.

"See," Geist said, stooping to the dust of the floor on the far side of the drawings Fred had spread out, "I became haunted by the form of that line, as I see it the leading edge of the butterfly's wing, the edge that gives it lift. For months I drew it even in my sleep. For you I make it in the dust so that you see it from the south. I am north."

Fred watched the line taking shape at the end of his yellowed index finger, beginning at his left, which Geist had said was west, as in the normal tradition of Western map-making. The line moved abruptly northeastward, then made a shallow turn southeast, then northeast again, still shallow, to a peak from which it declined rapidly, steeply, southeast a short distance, where it stopped. Geist left his finger at the end of the line he had drawn and said, "That's Geneva, on the southwest corner of Lac Leman. Switzerland. Neutral. The line stops at the French side of the border, at Crête de la Neige."

He traced his line back to its beginning at the foot of the southwestern leg. "We begin here, in the Pyrennes, at the Pic d'Orby. Pass north through Orthez, Mont de Marsan, so on—keep to the south and east of Tours, pass on through Bourges and here we are, look, where the line makes a crotch—this is Moulins. Then we go over toward Paray then north again through Chalon and so on—do you see?"

Well, not completely. Fred did not have a map of France in his head. He understood that the line was claiming a chunk of France, starting from the border with Spain at the southwest, and ending at the Swiss border.

"The *Line of Fat* is a delicate line. I chose fat for many reasons; not least was homage to my comrade, Joseph Beuys."

Fred said, "I should recognize this line?"

"Everyone wants it forgotten," Geist answered, his voice filled with a sudden eager passion. He rose with difficulty and wiped the dust from his fingers onto his pants. "Fifty some years ago that line was real enough. It could kill you. It was drawn by agreement between the invading Nazi power and the adventurers who formed the rule of Vichy. This border of collaboration was the price of the armistice of June 1940."

"It's not a line they print in the tourist guides," Fred said.

"On one side of the line the Germans ruled," Geist said. "And on the other, their French puppets and partners. The memory of much that happened along that line had been suppressed, like the line itself. Therefore I caused it to be drawn again, in fat."

Geist chuckled, rubbing out the line he had drawn, with his foot. "You see how easily it is gone," he said. "Diaspora of dust. My line of fat—because so many had gone hungry during the war, my first thought was a feast: of cheese, butter, lard, even sausage, to be laid across the land, floating where there was water. But that would have made a dotted line, as if the country were then to be torn along it; and I wanted a smooth ribbon, a good scar. Also I recalled that any use of pork or lard would offend the Jews, those who remain: which I did not wish to do. I decided on melted butter."

"It sounds expensive," Fred said. "Thousands of miles of butter? What would that cost?"

"It was a busy time for me," Geist said, shrugging the question off. "As you see from the last drawing, I was at the same time planning for the great work of 1994, only two years later." He whispered like an assassin and pointed toward the scribblings at the bottoms of the last two drawings in the pile, which were entirely different from the others. These two drawings presented variants of the straining vertical line that comes about when trapped forces of equal weight, such as bubbles, are thrusting against each other.

"For the five-hundredth anniversary of the Treaty of Tordesillas," Geist explained. "Which is the line the Pope drew in 1494, from the north to the south pole, across a globe whose size and shape he could not imagine. Look how it cleaves the Atlantic Ocean, chopping through Greenland, then later Brazil, which the Pope did not know existed. The mark was made by this Pope of Spain to separate the territories Spain was going to hijack out of the New World, from what Portugal, under both the Pope's and God's permission, would get license to rape."

"A line across the Atlantic Ocean?" Fred asked.

"If Pope Alexander VI could do it, why not Jacob Geist?"

Understanding this much of his man's cast of mind, Fred left the drawings where he had spread them and turned to the works in progress. Because all of the drawings focused on Tibet were inverted south-to-north, Fred gradually accepted the conclusion fostered by the artist's occasional annotations. The lower boundary of Tibet could be and, eventually, according to Geist, *must* be seen, as a skull cap in profile with its pronounced brow ridge occupying the borders with Burma and Szechwan.

"It shall be pollen, golden pollen," Geist had written below the drawing on which Fred had found the towns he had once visited (freezing, half-starved, and with his left arm in a sling of yak hair gunnysack). "Pollen shall fill the skull cup, making the mountains bloom."

"Fair enough," Fred said.

If the man had anything practical in mind, the size of this next ambition was simply staggering. True, France was large, neat, well regulated, and filled with busybodies; and its inhabitants could not have been friendly to the recreation of the Line of Demarcation, even though created of its favorite foodstuff. But given the right conditions, and financial backing, it was possible to conceive of the project's being carried out. Hadn't Christo wrapped the Pont Neuf?

As to the Treaty of Tordesillas cinquecentennial gesture: it might have been possible to execute that from a rented private jet—depending on what medium Geist had chosen for this line. But to accomplish anything in Tibet—apparently Geist's plan had been to inscribe his line of pollen along the former border between Tibet and China, some time during the year 2001: the fiftieth anniversary of the Chinese annexation of Tibet. Such a work would involve impossible logistics geographically. Tibet's mean altitude must be 15,000 feet, with glaciers and the world's worst maps and storms and mountains. Furthermore, given the region's politics, the wrong person wandering that part of the world today was simply throwing his life away.

"*Ha ko gee do*," Fred said. "I understand, Jacob, at least a little bit now, how your mind works; and it's an interesting mind, I'll give it that. The *Geistmaps* I love. But *deek song*, buddy. Enough already. If you fly even a foot into the air space China claims, you are dead meat."

But then, Jacob Geist was already dead meat, despite the lively intelligence of the work he'd left behind. The *Line of Golden Pollen* would not happen. It could not have happened anyway. The project would cost more than the war in Kuwait: both sides. It was a glaring and outrageous impossibility.

Fred laughed. The unlikeliness of the concept did not make it any less beautiful; nor did it diminish the intelligence or the beauty of the drawings. He gathered those he had spread out on the floor and, turning one over, noticed the printed label on the back of the acetate wrapping and read: THE ARMAND KORDERO GALLERY. The title, date, dimensions of the work had been typed onto the label, by Mirelle or her predecessor, as well as Kordero's inventory number, JG–53. The rest of the group carried Kordero labels also.

Chapter 11

"But I could not see a thing that attached him to the miniatures," Fred told Molly. "Cigarette butts and ashes and empty vodka bottles, yes: I found those in spades." He'd finally left Geist's studio at around nine o'clock, and called Molly from the first pay phone he could find. Not that he would have used it under the circumstances, but there had not been a telephone at Geist's place. Since the kids were doing a Saturday overnight with friends, Molly was free to join him at a halfway point, in Cambridge, where big women in red T shirts would feed Fred hamburgers while Molly toyed with something they claimed was a Margarita.

"At least if I decide to go back it'll be easier next time," Fred said. "I got the guy's spare keys. Bunch of them hanging next to the door. More than he needed to get in and out of the building and his studio space, so maybe he's got an apartment somewhere else; but the guy looked too poor."

Though there'd been no need for it, given the nature of their evening, Molly had gotten herself spruced up, even so far as to put on an unusual bright red lipstick that set off the deep yellow woolen dress she had chosen. Its color recalled the willow leaves that Fred had liberated from her dark curls last evening, in the yard.

The place Fred had picked was noisy, filled with law students who were trying to forget that they could have chosen to be something else.

Molly was unusually subdued this evening, as if the week had tired her out; or as if she hated the place they'd come; or as if she'd gotten a bill she couldn't understand, for something she didn't want.

"You read Sam's composition?" Fred asked.

"He says the snakes are your idea."

"In a manner of speaking, they were. Are."

"You might also tell him about the apostrophe that goes between t and s in what's, as in *What's in My Room.*"

"As long as you've got a pile of snakes, do you need apostrophes too?" Fred said. "Isn't that one of the rules of grammar?"

"I don't want that boy to go wild," Molly persisted. "He should take his work seriously. So should you, if you're going to get involved."

"I missed the apostrophe," Fred said.

The long pause that developed as Molly licked salt from the edge of her glass might be read as many observations on her part, including, *That's not all you missed, Fred.*

"Tell me about Jacob Geist," Molly demanded finally. "And if you care to, tell me what you plan to do."

If this was evasive action toward another patch of quicksand, Fred could join in the evasion. "Before I forget: with respect to the Line of Demarcation between Occupied France and Vichy during the war, do you recall the significance of November 11, 1992?" Fred asked.

Molly said, "No."

Fred said, "If ever I saw a man with a single-minded aim, it's Jacob Geist. He didn't live *for* his art; he *lived* his art and, as far as I could make out, he cared about nothing else, except alcohol and tobacco. It doesn't make sense that he was carrying that thing, that miniature, whatever it is. He worked, he slept, he ate—that's all I could see. A scattering of books he had, but nothing you could use to get a fix on what made him tick. The only art on his walls, even, was reproductions of wall paintings, cave paintings, from the Han period, I think. What he did to entertain himself, aside from looking out the window, I don't know. No radio or TV—*that* I can relate to. He had no refrigerator, but he certainly was living there. Beautiful, the work is, but I told you that already—so lively and robust and obstreperous and inventive.

"But no address book, so maybe he had it with him. But if so, they'd have used it to find someone who could point to where he lived. The place had no letters from friends or relatives, nothing in the wastebasket but wrappers and newspapers, not even bills. It's as if the man was in hiding. His dealer, Kordero, claimed not to know where he was, but a Kordero's going to say whatever suits the moment."

On the TV over the bar, on the far side of the noisy dining area where they were sitting, a wrestling match was taking place between two women, billed as the Blonde Bombshell and Mississippi Maude. The patrons filled the air with their advice to both contenders.

"Idiots," Molly said.

"I'm ordering more iced coffee," Fred said. "You want anything?"

"More salt," Molly said. "But they probably can't do that without dumping the drink. Coffee won't keep you awake?"

"Nothing I do is going to make a difference," Fred said, flagging a burly waitress. He asked for the refill of coffee, and a saucer of rock salt "for the lady. The kind they put around the rim of the glass, OK?"

"I'd order it if I wanted it," the lady in question remarked. "But thanks, I guess."

"As far as what I'm *going* to do about Jacob Geist, I don't know," Fred said. "We'll put the salt in a doggie bag and take it with us. I'm thinking, like the prudent conservator of paintings, don't do anything that's not reversible. It isn't my business to tell the authorities how to find out about Jacob Geist. If I do, and explain why I'm interested, I lose all control of events."

A cheer went up from the bar.

"I have a moral obligation to get that miniature to its owner," Fred said. "But I can't ask Geist who the owner is or was or should be now. I couldn't get a hint or a lead, at his place. Do I take the folio to customs or the cops? Not likely. Without knowing the rest of the story, I don't want to turn up out of the blue carrying something I can't explain. For all I know it's the well-known long-lost Boguslov Altarpiece from the cathedral of Saint Genasaria in Spinsk."

Molly rattled a straw in her crushed ice.

"I keep feeling there's something I'm not telling you," Fred said. "Or maybe it's vice versa. Do you get that feeling?"

"You were aware that Clayton invited Lakshmi Thomas to go to New Haven and watch him get his crown at Yale?" Molly asked.

"Well hey," Fred mused. "He's been more than usually obstinate and secretive. I thought he was out of joint about the manuscript, because he wants it so badly you can see it across the room. But even before I went to Paris on that wild goose chase…Heck, Molly, you think it's possible he's set his cap for Lakshmi? She's so in a different league! Beautiful, sexy, funny, young and smart…what would they have in common?"

"All I can say is he's taken her with him to Yale. They drove down together. You say you didn't know?"

"I knew there'd been talk of it last summer. They had, while we were working together on that thing, a certain— with a person of Clay's temperament I have a hard time finding words for it. I thought of Clay as overcome by a bewildered Platonic lust that dare not speak its name, or even look carefully at its object. While Lakshmi, who is a healthy woman, although she might have been briefly entertained by a passing attraction to occult…but no, it never occurred to me."

Molly wiped her mouth on a dinky pink napkin and began to smooth its crumpled paper again, punishing it against the black formica table top. The table rocked. "While you were in Paris, Lakshmi came by the house to show me the dress she planned to wear tonight, to the black tie do."

Molly paused.

"And?" Fred prompted.

"It fit," Molly said. "I have to say it fit. It'll do more for the occasion than spiking the punch with monkey glands."

"If he's, God help us, courting Lakshmi Thomas, I'm out of the woods," Fred said. "At least I can't imagine how he could chase both Lakshmi and that folio at the same time."

"It's not funny, Fred. If Clay doesn't, at least Lakshmi should have more sense."

"Lakshmi's a free agent," Fred said.

"I don't want Lakshmi hurt. She's half his age, and it's because of me she met him. Because of you."

"She's still a free agent," Fred said.

A cheer went up from the crowd at the bar. One of the wrestlers was pinned in a leg lock. The referee was counting her out.

"So much for the Blonde Bomber," Molly said. "Scratch another free agent. Fred, December-May's one thing, but Clay's an alien species."

"So if you cross a camel with a swan, at least offspring are unlikely," Fred said. "Oh, come on, Molly. Don't be mad. I won't make light of it if it's bothering you; but if it's true it's the first time since I've known him that Clayton even appeared to notice that a woman was a member of the opposite sex. That is, if you are right. You are so mad about it that you assume you're right, but we don't know. How do you…"

"We'll change the subject," Molly said. They sat in silence while Fred finished his coffee and Molly toyed with her dish of salt. Normally when they disagreed about something they fought it out if there was something one or the other of them could do about it. If there was nothing either could do concerning the subject at issue they argued as long as the subject entertained them, and then moved on. In this matter of Clay and Lakshmi, if Molly thought there was something Fred should do, she wasn't saying; and anyway both of them knew that Fred was not going to agree with her.

"Let me tell you about some of the jokers Armand Kordero has in his stable," Fred said.

"Over coffee. At least *I* want coffee," Molly said. "Somewhere else. Let's walk until we find a place that has grown-ups in it."

The moist air in Cambridge glistened with the city's lights. Molly took the arm Fred offered, although they did not normally impede each other's progress in this way, and together they poked along the sidewalk like tourists looking for a coffee shop in a strange land.

Chapter 12

In Molly's bed, next to a fitful Molly, Fred had slept fitfully until 4:30 a.m. They had, in fact, managed coffee at the place Molly chose in Cambridge; then they'd managed to be courteous to one another all the way to Arlington in Molly's Colt, with Fred crunched into the passenger seat. Then they had gone courteously to Molly's bedroom where they had lain courteously side by side. Any humane observer would have advised, if only in the interest of efficiency, that one of them ought simply to shoot the other and get it done.

Fred dressed and went downstairs, knocked around Molly's kitchen, failed to bring himself to the point of organizing coffee or breakfast, and went outside. The air was filled with the damp suspicion of impending sunlight. The birds who owned the street were already reminding each other of that fact. It was colder this morning, below sixty degrees, the first morning when the inevitability of winter had been apparent. Fred laid a hand on the hood of his old brown car and asked it, "You think you can make it back to Mexico, old girl, should the occasion arise?

"Bag this," he continued, and climbed in. Though he'd never bothered smoking, the previous tenant must have. The rusty fabric of the car's interior gave forth a familiar smell uncomfortably like that of Jacob Geist's place: an aura unsuited to the company of women.

"Come to think of it," Fred muttered, "nothing about Geist's studio, not even idle doodles in the dust, or on the dirty windows where steam from a boiling kettle would have made an attractive skrim of condensation, suggested any interest on Geist's part in the female phenomenon: not even the anatomical details that can preoccupy a man while he is thinking the fine thoughts he believes transport him away from the inscrutable sex. Nor were there graphic signals of interest in the inscrutable male sex—if *sex* is what I'm thinking. What did Geist do for company?"

Fred started his car and backed into the empty street. This part of Arlington was inhabited by sleeping families: the portion of civilization in whose behalf the rest of civilization committed its wars and mass starvations, its religious torments and suicidal agonies of philosophy or ecology.

Force had been Jacob Geist's obsession: the force that expresses itself by imposing and defending boundaries.

Fred drove until, in Medford, he found a diner he liked the look of. Inside, one man fried eggs and bacon and potatoes on the grill, while six men occupied seats at the counter. Fred nodded when he entered, because everyone turned toward him and nodded. None was a stranger to the other. All must be of the same tribe. The man in the white apron back of the counter knew that Fred wanted coffee and put it in front of him in a thick tan mug, asking, "Cream?"

"Fine," Fred told him, and ordered a large breakfast, number six.

Like Neanderthals discussing the group of Homo sapiens down the gorge, the men at the counter were discussing womankind, a species that had split off from their evolutionary tree at least a million years before. Having nothing to contribute, Fred half-listened to their conversation and half to a radio propped next to the coffee maker. The radio was wheezing local news stories interrupted by songs about tires and dental care.

"Just take the twentieth century," one of the men was arguing. "Name me one woman who can match your Stalin, your Hitler, your Mao, your Pol Pot, hell, even, I don't know, Ted Williams!"

"You think they never mated just because it didn't occur to them?" Fred asked.

He hadn't entered the conversation until now, and his sudden question threw everyone's timing off. "What do you mean, mating?" someone asked, as if he'd never run into the concept and needed it explained.

"Thinking about the tests they did, comparing the DNA," Fred explained. "The Neanderthal people and the Homo sapiens people, which we say is us, were living side by side in the same places for thousands of years, eating the same food, using the same tools, same clothes, wanting the same things—and all with the same physical equipment, you have to believe. Compatible genitals. And the scientists tell us there's no sign that they ever mated with each other."

"Three over easy," the counterman said, slapping Fred's plate down. "With ham."

"Your theory is, they could have, but it never crossed their mind?" one of the men asked. "Like the way between us and chimps nobody's ever tried? When there's guys will make it with sheep and chickens, and you hear of these films with women and dogs or mules?"

"Not a theory," Fred said. "More a question, an idle thought."

"Lions and tigers. They make it together," someone put in and started an argument that led to pod people and other science fiction. Fred's attention wandered from the conversation and toward the radio, the implications of whose observations about household murders and used car sales were more benign than the men's congenial ignorance, because it was heading in the direction of eugenics.

"The question in my mind is," Fred popped into a lull, "we take it for granted we're the group with family values, the ones who invented opera and cover-your-mouth-when-you-sneeze—the good guys. But the evidence is, isn't it? Since we're here and they're gone, and since we didn't mate and soak up each other's genes: we killed the Neanderthals, yes?"

Next thing you knew, someone suggested, a Senator was going to stand up in the Congress and demand that the President issue a formal apology to the Neanderthals.

From here this was going to go downhill into a patter of race-based jokes and slurs, because all of the diner's occupants were variants of the dominant mongrel breeds known in the States as *white*. If Fred stayed with the conversation he'd have to start teaching lessons to the invincibly ignorant. Behavior you might regulate by force or law, but not ideas. These were sweet, friendly men, and in their sweetness they would kill and maim and torment whomever it was in fashion to despise, just like any other men. Not that those friendly souls they killed or maimed would not return the favor, given the chance.

Fred turned his attention to the radio until he finished his third cup of coffee. He paid his bill, nodded to his fellows, and walked out.

⚊⚊⚊

The arrangement at the gray frame house on Chestnut Street in Charlestown was that someone remained awake at all times, sitting or standing watch at the desk, back of the front door. No one could sleep otherwise. Fred had not slept here in some time, though he kept a room for himself. As one of the building's three owners he liked to put his head in every few weeks, and he insisted on playing his part when it came to deciding who could stay here and—rarely—who must leave.

The occupants of the house were a pick-up group of veterans of this and that, military or clandestine services, who had learned that working within the friendly segments of society required talents their training had missed. Many who'd lived here had previously spent time on the streets. Some were being hunted, or thought they should be. For most the house provided a secure place in which to get their bearings while the demands of justified paranoia became less pressing. Some stayed for a while, speechless, and then disappeared into the wilderness again. Asking no questions was an important part of the drill. For those who knew the answers to the questions, it was likely expedient not to answer. So it wasn't a friendly group. But there was occasional comradeship around the pool table in the common room, and a few strong alliances had begun here. Mostly, the men kept to themselves until they were ready for the next stage, which might be practicing medicine again, or driving the crosstown bus in Topeka, or going home to an abandoned wife and children to tell them, "I'm home," or "I divorce you"; or finishing themselves off.

The man at the desk this morning was Jackie Banner. He was broadly bearded, wore his black hair wild, and could have played the role of Edward Teach. In his ragged lumber-jack shirt he looked incongruous where he sat, reading the paper, under a large Jane Peterson still life of zinnias. Fred, having come into the picture almost accidentally, had hung the painting there to subdue the men by making them confront Peterson's hint of the terrors of domestic life.

After they had exchanged greetings, Fred sat on the orange vinyl chair they kept here for visitors.

"Reynolds," Fred said. "Someone should mention to Rusty that around here you don't ask a person, 'You in trouble?'"

"Shit," Jackie said, and glanced nervously over his shoulder at Peterson's zinnias. "The place has two rules. No women, and mind your business. That's two more rules than Reynolds can remember. He can't count his own asshole. The guy..." Jackie Banner looked fearfully behind him.

"He said there was someone looking for me yesterday."

"Didn't mention it to me." Jackie Banner yawned, airing the spaces between large yellow teeth. "But I haven't seen

Reynolds. I took over after Teddy's shift. Teddy's back, by the way, but he's not too bad. He's sacked out in your room. It's where he thinks he goes."

"The guy looking for me," Fred said. "I hoped Rusty would leave word. If he shows up again, and if you all don't mind offering him hospitality until I can get here, I'd like to talk to him."

Chapter 13

"What else am I going to do on a Sunday morning, go to the dog races?" Hannah Bruckmann asked.

"I planned to put a message on your tape," Fred said. "Not expecting you to be in your office—in case you had any preliminary insight…"

"Come if you're free," Hannah Bruckmann said. "I'm on the third floor. The guard rings me and I let you in."

"What time?" Fred asked.

"I'm here now. Pick up a cup of tea and any kind of muffin without raisins or nuts or garbage in it. An honest muffin, if you can find one."

"Give me a half hour," Fred said, and passed the telephone back to Jackie Banner. On an impulse he'd called from the desk at Chestnut Street. "Three thirty-three Washington. That's the Jeweler's Building, isn't it?" Fred asked.

"I wouldn't know," Jackie Banner told him and went back to the Business section.

Since the Jeweler's Building is in the heart of Boston's downtown commercial area, nine on a Sunday morning was not a bad time to find a parking place. Plenty of spaces offered themselves with meters that would be irrelevant until Monday morning. Fred docked his car near the old Jordan Marsh, now Macy's, crossed the somnolent and almost deserted intervening space, and approached the Jeweler's Building's Sunday security, which allowed him access to the elevator only after the armed guard had conferred on the intercom with Hannah Bruckmann.

She met him at the elevator, looking first to the paper bag he carried from Chico's. She was dressed in blue jeans and a large brown sweater with twigs and snags caught in it. Like the muffin she didn't want, it looked like something with lots of roughage you'd buy from a save-the-world catalog whose main purpose pretended to be the preservation of threatened cottage industry in the Falkland Islands.

"They swear it's a plain muffin with nothing in it except muffin," Fred said. He followed her along a corridor whose closed doors carried lettering identifying the proprietors and specialties of the establishments: findings, precious stones, appraisals, supplies, wedding rings, certified diamonds, watches, repairs.

"Sundays I collate," Hannah Bruckmann said, stopping abruptly and applying her keys to the double locks of the door whose glass panel identified the shop inside as BRUCKMANN BOOKS.

"It's quiet Sunday mornings. Collating is like anything else where you have to keep track. Make a mistake, you can buy a book that's missing a gathering. Call me Hannah. If you can influence that other man, Clayton Reed, get him to do the same. He won't stop calling me Ms. Bruckmann. Come on in."

Bruckmann Books was a windowless room twenty feet square, all of its walls filled by shelves crammed with books and objects, like clay tablets, that bore words in other than book format. Tables down the center of the room carried more books, some closed, some lying open on stands that allowed the display of pages with illustrations. The place was a controlled riot of the printed and painted word. Hannah's desk, at the far end of the room, was piled with still more books.

"Take a chair," Hannah invited. She made room for the bag from Chico's by pushing aside the opened volume she had been studying. Removing the cover from the carton of tea, she went on, "We don't want to drip on a first edition of Fracastoro's *Syphilis Sive Moribus Gallicus*; Verona, 1530—even if it's missing a leaf, J-4."

Fred sat on the small hard chair that she had indicated was to be his punishment for disturbing her Sunday morning count.

"But it's *not* missing J-4," Hannah said. "The seller was careless and leaped to the wrong conclusion. That means he short-changes himself by five figures. J-4's not missing, it just got bound in with L. That won't mean anything to you, Fred, but don't mind me. I like to crow when someone else's stupidity makes me a better profit. If he tells me the book's deficient, and sets his price accordingly, that's his lookout."

"Clayton Reed's been calling you?" Fred asked.

Hannah broke her muffin open, looked for unwanted contaminants, found none, and took a bite. "He called twice yesterday," she said. "Very polite, and not wanting to rush me. He's anxious for information. You seem to be also, Fred."

"Beyond I know what I like, I'm lost in the field," Fred admitted.

"You know nothing about rare books?"

Fred shook his head.

"And nothing about the history of what you showed me?"

Fred continued shaking his head.

"It's more the history of the twentieth century that's at issue," Hannah said. "Before the first world war, nothing that's in this room would have been any big deal, not financially, not even the Gutenberg Bible on the top shelf over there. That Catalan *Book of Hours* from about 1500, really beautiful, with a provenance that hasn't got a hole in it anywhere—breathtaking miniatures—that book cost me over a hundred thousand bucks. And it'll bring me a profit of twenty thousand." She pointed toward an illuminated text laid open on a stand on the room's central table. Fred had to turn to see it. The book measured something like seven by five inches.

"The market's become nothing you could have imagined a hundred years ago," Hannah continued. "You might have spent a thousand dollars on the thing in 1910, talking today's dollars, not the dollars of 1910, when a thousand dollars was serious money. What you get for a thousand today you could have had back then for sixty-two, give or take; and depending what you were buying. Old books? I'm wrong, you could likely get the same thing for ten. My point is, there's a market now where there didn't use to be one.

"The rare book business, to simplify, was the invention of Austrian Jews, starting before the first World War. My father did not enter it until between the wars, when he was a young man of twenty, in Vienna.

"You don't need me to tell you what happened in Europe, or to the Jews of Europe, during the nineteen hundreds. However, at the same time as the currencies of many nations were going to hell, especially in the twenties, when everyone's money just blew up, some things not only held their value— their value increased like lightning. This happened with paintings as you know, which are a Gnostic substitute for currency. But it's true also with books. Because even before the first war, certain rich old men, many of them in this country, fought to outbid each other for such things and assemble the best collections. As time went by and we got into the twenties and thirties, their competition drove the values up at the same time as competition on the ground in Europe, then in Asia, drove the value of human life down to, sometimes, less than the human body's worth as fuel.

"Book traders or collectors in Europe, in 1939 and 1940, especially if they were Jews, set out to distill, that is to decrease the size and weight of their collections. They traded bulk against rarity in order, when they could, to arrive at a single precious object having the same worth as a whole collection, but which might be, for example, sewn into the lining of a coat so it could be brought out of danger and sold in the free world for whatever fortune it might command."

Hannah had been fiddling with the plastic container of cream while she talked. She opened it and dumped it into her tea. She looked up at Fred, who shook his head, and then she began to stir it with a pencil which she licked afterwards. "Diamonds show up on X-rays," she said. "The Nazis soon learned to X-ray the clothing and the persons of those emigrating or being interned, so that they could cut out what they wanted. You know all this. So when I looked at the folio in Mr. Reed's beautiful room yesterday, so comfortable and so filled with precious objects, the first thing I wondered was, where's the dead Jew? Because such a folio would have been perfect as a means to coalesce a family's treasure, back in 1939. What it was worth then I can't really say. If it is what I think, today it's worth about a million dollars. I know one collector who would pay a million and a half for it."

"You told Clay Reed?" Fred asked after a moment's pause.

"I wasn't sure, and I am not sure." Hannah took a drink and ate the rest of her muffin while Fred looked over the glaring new landscape she had exposed.

"You said, if it's what you think it is," Fred interjected. "What do you think it is?"

"There's more work to be done," Hannah said. "Also, to be prudent, I should look at the object again."

"If we're talking that kind of value, in fairness to you, you should know more," Fred said. "I have custody of the manuscript by accident. The person who last had it is out of reach. Can you learn where it comes from?"

"No one will tell you its history?" Hannah insisted.

Fred spread his arms.

"It's a major undertaking. I want five thousand dollars to do the research. I'll have to see the folio again. Say tonight?

At five? I'll collect a check at the same time. I want to buy the thing, and if I do your money will be refunded, along with a finder's fee. In the meantime, if you can, prevent the disbursement of the other leaves of this book, and keep them off the market. Rarity is premium. Do you agree?"

"Oh, sure," Fred said.

"Then I'll start turning over rocks."

Fred stood. "Where would you go to sell a thing like that?" he asked. "Besides the auction houses?"

"That is my business."

"My question is, the person who had it: where might he or she have been going?"

Hannah said, "Indeed."

Chapter 14

"Thought you and the kids might join me," Fred told the phone, "or else I'll join you."

"You say you're in Boston?" Molly asked.

"At Clayton's, as I told you," Fred said. "Let's have brunch on Charles Street or walk over and do the swan boats before they're put away for the winter, or…"

"I didn't know where you were," Molly said. "We didn't have plans. Not knowing when you might surface again, I told Ophelia we'd join her in Lincoln and canoe on her river. We meaning the only we I can speak for, my children and me."

"Point noted," Fred said. "Didn't you get my message?"

"Fred, I don't mean to be cross. For all I knew you'd gone back to New York. All your note says is that you'll call before noon. Meanwhile my sister asked us for brunch or lunch or whatever the hell she has in mind, and she's got my mother coming also, and I said yes. It's not a big deal. Come join us."

"I'm to meet someone here at five," Fred said. "Hannah Bruckmann, the rare book dealer. I have to pass. Let Sam hold up the honor of the male persuasion on his own, unless Ophelia's landed someone. Anyway, I'm sorry. I'm not much of a guest or companion or lover."

Molly said, "You left a nice note."

"I did?"

"The second sentence; where it said, 'I'll see you tonight.'"

"It's not poetry," Fred said.

"No. It's much better. You do what you're doing. I'm sorry about last night. I just…"

"I know," Fred tried, and waited for Molly's eventual, "See you tonight, then," which sounded more like, *You don't seem to. You don't seem to know anything.*

Fred whacked down the phone and went to Clayton's street floor living area. He hadn't had a chance to study the parchment on his own; hadn't even laid eyes on it since Friday afternoon. He was approaching the piano, reaching to whisk back the protective cloth Clayton had placed over the folio, when the doorbell rang.

On the other side of the front door's peephole a middle-aged male stranger occupied thirteen hundred dollars worth of suit. He had found a sweeping blond beach-boy haircut to go with it. Fred opened the door an inch.

"George Szefris," the man told Fred, thrusting a card toward him.

"You are lost?" Fred asked.

"May I come in?"

"Of course not."

The man had placed a black leather overnight case on the stoop next to his unobtrusively ferociously expensive shoes, so as to keep his hands free for greeting and thrusting cards. Fred stepped outside and closed the door on them both. "Your business?" Fred asked.

"Rare books, incunabula, miniatures," George Szefris said.

"Too bad," Fred told him.

The man's smile gleamed as if each tooth had been hand-crafted by an expert. "My appointment is not until Tuesday morning," he said. "But I was so excited I could not wait."

Fred promised, "You'll wait. Appointment with whom? About what?"

"You are not Clayton Reed?" Szefris asked with relief.

"What time Tuesday morning?" Fred asked.

George Szefris raised his eyebrows and his bag and carried them all down the stairs. He turned at the end of the walk and asked, "What hotel do you recommend?"

"I don't," Fred said. "It makes all the others jealous." He locked himself into the house again and muttered, "Clay, you idiot, what are you doing? Knowing how fast the grapevine works in a tiny world, did you ask for a second opinion? When it's my business to begin with? What does Clay want, a cloud of vultures circling his house?"

As he crossed Clay's parlor again the phone rang. "You want to come over?" Teddy's voice asked from Chestnut Street.

"Talk to you later," Fred told the hidden parchment, placing his hand briefly on its cover. He checked the security sensors and left the building by Clayton's street door, pulling it fast behind him as he turned to descend the stairs. A young man in twenty-five hundred dollars worth of blue suit, and with a sweep of discreet tan hair to set it off, was turning into Clay's walk from Mountjoy Street. His taxi pulled away from the curb and rolled downhill toward Charles through a pattering swirl of golden leaves.

"Perfect timing," the young man rejoiced. "Mr. Clayton Reed, I presume."

"You do," Fred said, taking the frank slim hand as it was offered, and noting the glint of perfect light from its beautiful fingernails.

"Simeon Simplex," the young man said beaming a smile from which new luxury cars streamed forth with all the accessories. "Hearst Museum, Los Angeles."

"The *wunderkind*," Fred recalled aloud. The young man simpered, unable to deny the compliment all the newspaper art critics had given him six months back when his rumored appointment was confirmed.

Simeon Simplex thrust himself closer to Fred and confided, "Yesterday evening I called an emergency meeting with my board's executive committee, in time for me to catch the red-eye. Stopped only long enough to bathe at the Ritz and change my grubby clothes. May I come in?"

"No," Fred said.

"I have emergency authorization to commit the Hearst Museum to purchase," he dropped his voice to a thrilling hush, "the object," his voice ascended again to normal range, "pending examination by our curator, who arrives from London within the hour. The funds are appropriated. They can be wired at a moment's notice, even today, Sunday. It is all arranged. Under my direction, it is how the museum has learned that it must function in today's climate. The Hearst, as you know, although we started late in the game, is committed to assembling a collection that rivals those of the Cloisters, the Morgan, the Beineke, Houghton..."

"I'm meeting someone," Fred said, pulling away. "If you want to visit, ride a couple blocks with me. Where you headed?"

Fred led the way to his car, explained that the passenger door in front would not close again if he were to open it, and made room on the back seat for Simeon Simplex. "Where to?" he asked again once he had persuaded the engine to respond to the ignition key.

"What time is convenient?" Simeon Simplex asked. "Giuseppe Broggi's plane arrives Logan at 2:00. Our arrangement is for him to meet me at your home once he clears customs. There's a limousine waiting. Broggi, you know, is our new curator of medieval manuscripts. I fired the old one. It was among my first acts as director. I am determined all my staff at the Hearst will be aggressive. You have an appointment. We can put our meeting off until, shall we say, four o'clock? Is that convenient?"

Fred shook his head.

"What then, six? Or—I know—perfect! You'll dine with us! They are saving a table for me at Langosto's. Eight o'clock."

"Tell you what, Simplex, why don't you climb out here? I'm going to go with Sam Fogg, or the Getty. You're at the Ritz? I'll call if I change my mind."

"Don't be fooled," Simeon Simplex warned. "The Getty romances you and strings you along and meanwhile they've got their army out looking higher up the pipe. They'll find your source and cut you out. As to Sam Fogg, that firm's a friend and I won't cast aspersions. They handle fine things. I buy there. I think the world of Sam Fogg. We all do. But I hear they're so overextended now…"

"I'll be off," Fred said.

"Make no commitments until you have our offer," Simeon Simplex pressed. "With Hearst, you have our whole legal staff to rely on, also. We don't, in a case such as this, even expect the seller to guarantee clear title, as the Getty might. There's…"

"Out," Fred said.

"They said you were prickly, Reed," Simeon Simplex muttered, wrestling with the door. "I would have telephoned, but your number is not listed."

"True," Fred said. He backed out of Clayton's double parking space and, in his rear-view mirror, watched Simeon Simplex staring at his exhaust. "Twerp," Fred said. "Nobody's crossed him since fourth grade. Born rich, as you must be if you're going to run a big museum, wonder boy has dressed and smiled and slept his way into the arms of the Hearst's trustees and anything else he wants."

Traffic between Boston and Charlestown was sporadic and uninteresting. Nothing of moment was happening in Boston on this Sunday afternoon. To the disgust of Sam and Terry, the Red Sox had blown their chances once again, and only strangers were left in contention. Nobody cared who claimed the pennant.

Fred drove across the bridge wondering, "Who's Sam Fogg?"

Across from the place on Chestnut Street, and a little way down the block, a rusted white Taurus wagon sat with its nose against a pile of leaves some children had been assembling a few days before. Fred took a note of its license number as he strolled over to look at the vehicle, whose driver surged out and made for him in a flurry of threat....

Chapter 15

....to break arms, head, legs, ribs, neck—whatever came handy.

"What you want with my number? What you want with my number? What you want with my license number?" the big man demanded, jabbing both fists against Fred's chest in the quick tattoo that provokes hasty response in a bar room brawl. Skinny hips, wide shoulders, brown hair down the neck, square face, clean-shaven...

Fred stepped back and sideways, dodging. "John Travolta?" he asked.

"You Fred?" Travolta asked, letting his fists down slightly. "What you want with my license?"

"Just instinct," Fred said, tearing up the paper and dropping the fragments into the breeze, which carried them toward the leaf pile.

"We'll sit in my car," Travolta said.

"Probably not," Fred amended. "Nothing wrong with the front stairs." He led the way to the house he did not call home and sat on the top step, patting the tread next to him. "What's on your mind?"

The man who had borrowed John Travolta's name, and someone else's Northeastern University sweatshirt, stood on the sidewalk facing Fred, his hands on his hips. He stared, chewing his lower lip, measuring relative weights and distances, figuring odds and angles. "Geist. Guy called Jacob Geist. Where is he?" Travolta said.

Fred scratched his face. "Who wants to know? is my question," Fred answered. "Aside from yourself?"

Travolta said, "I want Geist. That simple enough?"

"There I can help you. His dealer in New York—Jacob Geist is an artist," Fred started. "—is Armand Kordero. That's who I talked to. On 57th Street. I can give you Kordero's number."

"I don't need it," Travolta said. "You live in this house? Place is a shithole." Travolta stared menacingly long enough to learn that Fred would not argue the other side of this proposition. Then he turned and went back to his car. Fred watched the white Taurus wagon jerk and drive away, bouncing.

"Kordero's not fooling around," Fred said. "Not if he can send a man to check out my address within hours of my giving it to him. Geist was his courier? How does that make sense if Kordero had lost touch with the old boy—which may or may not be true. No. Hold it. Don't start drawing conclusions and erecting fictions just because you have the urge to string together the few things you know and make them into a coherent pattern. Invention makes problems."

Fred went into the house, saying hello to Teddy, who had come to the door through whose window panels he could keep track of the source and direction of the conversation outside. Teddy wore a black suit a size or two too large for him, and a white shirt that was freshly ironed. He looked like a seminarian who has been fasting for forty days.

Fred told him, "Thanks for calling."

"Man didn't want to wait inside," Teddy said. His look was not so much frantic as haunted. The cards he'd been dealt placed him in one of the mongrel groups Americans call *black*, which gave him that much more to get past if he was going to manage in the world. In the meantime he was inventive and dependable around the place in Charlestown, though he sometimes disappeared for months. It was not prudent, but Fred had developed a great affection for the man.

"Reckon he likes his car better," Fred said. "He tell you anything? Like who he's with, or where he's from?"

Teddy shook his head and sat at the desk. Fred pulled the phone toward him and punched the numbers that got him Dee's answering machine in Cambridge. "Dee, do me a favor. Run Mass plate number 193-123 and tell me what you get. Or, no, call Molly and tell her. I don't know where I'll be."

He hung up, telling Teddy, "She's a meter maid for Cambridge. She can send a number to the Registry on that box she carries, and find things out."

Teddy nodded and looked away. It was none of his business.

Fred said, "I'm going to leave my car out front while I take a walk."

Teddy said, "Watch your back."

Fred sauntered along Arnold Street. If the authorities had put the matter on a front burner, they should have found Geist by now, and be making the street nervous with their vehicles. But there was no sign of interest or action at Number Seven. Fred walked past the building, stretched his legs for another two hundred yards, then doubled back. The neighborhood was enjoying a quiet afternoon.

The door next to the Lovett Shoe building's loading dock was locked. Having Geist's spare keys now, Fred did not need to waste time letting himself inside. Geist's studio was as he'd left it the evening before. No one had been here in the meantime doing whatever people do when they break into a dead man's place.

Fred boiled water in the old man's kettle, washed a cup, and made tea from the supply of tea bags he'd found in a paper bag near the hot plate. He carried his cup to the rocking chair and sat gazing out the windows while the tea steeped. There was nothing to see but sky and the dirt on the glass, which caused a mottling that looked like dingy clouds that would shift in any direction the watcher directed simply by tilting his head the opposite way.

"Here's where we are, Jacob," Fred said. "The parchment you were carrying is, and/or represents, a treasure of magnitude. Fact one. Three people know more about it than I do: Hannah Bruckmann; George Szefris from New York; and the director and executive committee of the Hearst Museum. That's fact two." He drank tea and rocked as Jacob Geist must have done here, staring out the window when there was rain, or snow, or darkness, or dawn over the Navy Yard. Where were Geist's friends, lovers, children?

"Fact three. Kordero is so anxious to find you that he sicced a goon on me, on the off chance that I knew something. Those are the facts I have. There's so much surmise struggling for my attention that I can barely keep it from parading itself as facts. Surmise one: most obvious and cruel—Jacob Geist was a poor man. Therefore he had no right to carry something worth a fortune. To which I counter yes, but he's an artist so all bets are off. If his own art represents a fortune, it never did to him. The way he lived proves he defies commercial values.

"But explain Kordero's goon."

Fred put what he did not know aside, among the guesses he wanted to make. He finished his tea. He washed the cup and set it upside down in a dirty saucer to drain dry. Then he went to the drafting tables to enjoy Geist's work again.

"Or *these* few dots of fact could signal the ghostly boundary of some story," Fred speculated, considering the intricately worked map fragments. "Another fact is, Geist is dead. This project he was working on is fact, which was well along, at least in the artist's speculation. The work is intended to embarrass the People's Republic of China, which does not suffer humiliation gladly. If China had wind of the plan—why not a Chinese agent behind him at Logan, with a cyanide tipped dart....?"

Who'd been around them in the crush of passengers leaving the Paris plane? Who, besides Fred, had been in a position to do the old man mischief?

"Get information. Don't speculate," Fred said. He looked once again around the studio. The smell of the cigarette butts; the mattress and blankets—all were eloquent of the old man's mortal presence, but they would not reveal where he had been or what he planned to do.

"So, we talk to the neighbors," Fred decided.

The rest of the third floor was empty, the office doors either being open on vacant space, or padlocked closed. What were the names of the other tenants in the building? Beamer, yes; and Katz/Moncrieff. One of them had sounded like fun yesterday afternoon.

"That'll have to wait," Fred said. He'd lost track of the time. It was four o'clock now. Hannah Bruckmann was scheduled to meet him at five on Beacon Hill. Before that, he'd do well to telephone Clayton Reed at the hotel in New Haven and tell him, "Look, Clay, going into your second childhood's all very well. But if you want to impress Lakshmi Thomas, turn somersaults for her, or talk Latin. Don't brag about my parchment folio in front of a cocktail party filled with all the whoozits and kissmyasses of the art world. Word's getting around, and Hannah Bruckmann didn't start it.

"Correction: did I say *my* parchment, Jacob? I didn't mean that, but—well, you know how it is."

Chapter 16

"Mr. Reed, my card." The man smiled, throwing open the driver's door of Fred's car. While Fred was parking the fellow had slid across Mountjoy Street, emerging from the magnolia shadows on the far side so fast that Fred had barely seen him coming. The man looked pacific enough. He might not need his arm broken, not yet. Still....

"Back off," Fred said.

"Calpagian," the man insisted warmly, though he recoiled slightly. "Stanley Calpagian. Hear me out."

Fred climbed from his car and made a show of locking it, even though anything that might get into it from the outside was worth more than the car was.

"Counselor at law," Calpagian said. He was dressed for golf, but carried both a rolled umbrella and a briefcase in one hand. "Speed, in a case like this, can be of the essence," Calpagian insisted. "Hear me out, sir. I have a world of experience in these matters."

"Las Vegas?" Fred asked, glancing at the man's business card before he stuffed it into his shirt pocket. "You've dropped in from Las Vegas, Nevada?"

"Got a call on my car phone and made a screaming instant U turn. That's how I am," Calpagian boasted.

Fred leaned against the car and folded his arms. "You got a call," he repeated. "Who from, counselor?"

Despite the fact that he was dressed for golf, white shoes and all, Calpagian wore an embroidered polo player with a horse on his yellow knit shirt. He picked at the emblem while he studied the ethics of his position.

"You're here to solicit business," Fred prompted. "I've got a lot of company all of a sudden. Who called you?" He smiled the smile that Molly had asked him not to use within three blocks of the library where she worked.

"No reason in the world I shouldn't tell you. I'm breaking no confidence. Ben Marlowe. Friend of yours. Small world. Friend of mine too. Knowing my success in similar instances, Ben Marlowe asked me to drop everything and fly out to give you a hand, Mr. Reed."

So there was one question answered. Clay's pal Marlowe, in addition to vouching for Hannah Bruckmann, had set off the present avalanche. Fred said, "Reed isn't here. Not in Boston. Not in the state."

"That's wise," Calpagian blurted, nodding eagerly. "I told him, I said, Marlowe, tell your man to take that thing immediately to Switzerland. Otherwise it's a rat's nest. That was my advice, which Reed followed. Good start. Then you're Fred Taylor, the assistant. Excellent. I'll meet Reed in Switzerland. What city? What hotel?

"See the thing is, as I told Ben Marlowe, in Switzerland the property laws are in our favor. Get the thing to Switzerland right away. See, in Switzerland, if you can hold onto anything long enough to say 'It's mine' three times, that about does it for Switzerland. So already on account of my advice we have the protection of Swiss law, whereas, if we try to operate out of this country we have to work around the National Stolen Property Act, and also the 1970 UN Treaty on Cultural Property, which can be a bear. Terrific. I mean there's not a chance we're not talking at least war booty at some point in the past, whatever Mr. Reed's present good-faith title situation may be. No? What hotel did you say?"

"Intercontinental. Geneva," Fred said. "He's using the name Himmler. Henry Himmler."

"Great. Tell him I'll meet him for breakfast. I've gotta make tracks. He does have the complete manuscript with him?"

"I pass messages along," Fred said. "I don't originate them. I tell Mr. Reed we talked, he takes it from there."

"Fast as Reed moves, we'll make a great team," Calpagian said. "I'm going to enjoy this. Tell you what, Fred. I'll stay at the Intercontinental too, make it simpler. Tell him to do nothing until we confer, enjoy the lake, whatever they have there, lake, isn't it? Tell him…or shall I telephone him from here?"

"Better you speak to him in person," Fred advised.

Calpagian grasped Fred's hand in both of his, picked up the umbrella and the bag he'd dropped in order to execute this maneuver, grinned, and scuttered out of the story.

"Holy mackerel," Fred said, trotting down the stairs to his basement. He locked himself in, deactivated the alarms, and went to the ringing telephone. The cow in the small Church landscape, in its pasture of innocence, lowed, "moo-oose."

"Yes?" Fred asked.

"This is Cleveland Riggs' office, in Chicago?" a personable female voice told him, "with a call for Mr. Clayton Reed. If you have not already spoken with Dr. de Hamel…"

"My client will speak to no one," Fred announced and unplugged the phone. "No, wait a minute, there's Molly," he amended; connected the phone again and called her number. He waited out Sam's joke, *You have the right to remain silent*…until he could record, "Molly, I'm at Clay's but not answering the phone. I'll call you at six o'clock, and then every hour on the hour until I reach you."

Clayton Reed was not in his room at the Royal Court Hotel New Haven. The desk did not know where he was and would not divulge it if they did. They accepted, with ill-concealed reluctance, Fred's dictated message. *Ben Marlowe*

blabbed big time. Tell him to bag it. But it's too late. Enjoy.
Fred.

He checked his watch and looked out front in time to see Hannah Bruckmann pay her driver and sprint up the walk as the taxi behind hers disgorged a dapper old man who tossed bills through the window at his driver and followed as close behind her as his cane allowed.

"You brought a friend," Fred observed, blocking the doorway.

"No friend of mine," Hannah said. "He picked me up at my building. He's bad news."

"Inside," Fred said, and closed her in. He walked down the stairs to Clayton's brick walk, hailing the old man's taxi; took this visitor by the gray suit jacket with the pin stripe, turned him, and led him back to the street. The old man, out of breath, was doing his best to speak.

"Write me at this address," Fred said and handed the man one of the day's collection of strangers' business cards from the cache that had been building in his shirt pocket. He opened the taxi door and saw the old man inside. "Take it away, Mac," he told the driver.

Hannah was waiting in the hallway behind the front door. She'd been watching through Clayton's peep hole. "I'm embarrassed," she said, worrying at some roughage in her brown sweater. "I never thought to look behind me: didn't know he was there until I was paying my driver, and by then it was too late."

"He's bad news?" Fred prompted. "How bad? Bad news for whom?"

"Can we sit down?" Hannah asked. Under his feet, Fred noticed the new shuffle of pasteboard cards that had been pushed through the mail slot while he was out this afternoon, like windblown leaves. He stuffed them into his shirt pocket with all the others as he led Hannah along the hall and into the cool dimness of Clayton's parlor.

"Did you forget your bag in the taxi?" Fred asked. Hannah shook her head, patted a hip pocket, and sat in the chair Clayton Reed liked to pontificate from, where she'd seen him last Friday evening.

"I don't know how that shit got onto me," Hannah said. "I apologize in advance because I promise you there is going to be trouble. I was cagey as hell, but I can't do your work without asking questions: at Chantilly, the Cloisters, the Bibliothèque Nationale in Paris—it could not be avoided. It's always a risk. This world's so tight, and no one in it makes an honest living. I mean librarians and curators and functionaries are given piss poor wages, and if you're in business like me, high risk, you've got to nail the occasional huge outrageous profit or go under. How did you ditch him so fast?"

"More to the point," Fred said, "whom did I ditch?"

"Philippe de Houley," Hannah said. "He bills himself as a lawyer-aesthete. In fact he's an ambulance chaser. He's one of those French counts that gets born with a name and no money, but lots of old furniture and an address in the right Paris neighborhood he can't afford either to keep up or to give up, since if he gave it up, who would he be? So he plays the international game on a shoestring, keeps his eyes and ears open, and has a hundred thousand extra eyes and ears working for him. His specialty's rare books and the other works of art that were raided and raped and traded and stolen and sold and hidden and forged and destroyed in Europe during and after the Second World War. War loot, in short. Or anything of the kind in private or public hands where the title might have a shadow on it.

"Philippe de Houley smells these things out, then offers himself for hire to a credible alternate claimant, and makes trouble until he's got a settlement, or a suit, or a finder's fee, or a private treaty sale, or a bribe, or a hefty reward—in two cases I know of, from both sides of the ownership contention he started himself. Don't smile. Next thing you know, he'll knock at your door with a bailiff, a subpoena, and a posse behind him, and he'll be representing the French Ministry for Cultural Affairs, and demanding the *Limbourg Bible* of Philip the Bold."

Chapter 17

"That's what you've got. I'm sure of it," Hannah said. "Show me that folio again."

They crossed to the grand piano and Fred peeled back the cover. The skin lay with its *Lazarus* miniature up: despair and hope and joy and midsummer harvest all at once.

Hannah said, "This pressed for time, I just don't know. The boys in the business all agree the *Lazarus* was by Herman. Let me think about this." She continued to worry at her sweater while she worked, running her eyes across the painting with great care.

"Clue me in," Fred suggested. "Unless it was a for-instance, you bounced in with a complete blue-eyed story. What is the story? Meanwhile all the wild dogs of civilization are gathering in the shadows at the edge of the clearing, or calling, or marching up to the front door showing their beautiful teeth. I've got to make some decisions soon. I mean, in minutes. Tell me—you're serious when you say the Limbourg brothers? They painted the Duke of Berry's *Book of Hours*, am I right? How many brothers were there? I never noticed."

"Real quick," Hannah said, not taking her eyes off the painting, "When they were born I don't know. Nobody does. They came from Guelders, over on the German side of France, a town called Nimwegen. Apparently, that's how they came to be called the Limbourg brothers. You explain it. Their uncle, their mother's brother, was a painter who, by 1397, had been hired by one of the big guns in the royal house of France, Philip the Bold, the Duke of Burgundy. In those days, you were the Duke of it, you owned it. Take notes if you want to remember this. I hate to repeat myself.

"Being a king's son, and king's brother, and uncle of kings, Philip the Bold did what he wanted in life. He kept castles everywhere including in Paris, which is where this painter uncle, named Malwell—*Paint-well.* Sounds like the Ozarks, doesn't it?—was working. We know Malwell had arranged for two of his nephews, John and Herman, to be apprenticed to a goldsmith in Paris. Paul, the older brother, wherever he was at this time, everyone agrees was the best painter— but I'm getting ahead of myself.

"In Paris in 1399 there was a plague that was serious enough so that the goldsmith sent the two brothers, John and Herman, back home. Unwisely, they took a detour to Brussels, were caught up in a tug of war between Guelders and I forget what, with the result that the two so-called boys—probably they were in their late teens or even older— were jailed and held for ransom. That ransom was paid by the uncle's patron, the Duke of Burgundy, Philip the Bold. As a result of this act of mercy, Philip the Bold more or less owned them.

"Now. We know from house accounts that by 1402–3, Philip the Bold had hired both John and his older brother, Paul, at 20 Parisian cents a day (which wasn't much—maybe a little better than our minimum wage), to make the pictures for a beautiful and noteworthy Bible. I quote: '*pour faire les ystoires d'une belle et très notable Bible.*'

"That Bible's what you've got. I'm certain.

"Philip the Bold died in 1404. The Bible simply disappeared. No one has even been able to say with certainty that it was completed. A project that size—the two brothers had been hired for four years just to do their part, the pictures and initials and so on. Philip was dead before it could have been finished.

"Here's a detour, and it's about value. You recall the *Gospels of Henry the Lion?*"

"I can't say I do," Fred said.

"Sold at auction at Sotheby's in London in 1983 for twelve million dollars. It was said then to be 'the finest illuminated manuscript in private hands. But the manuscript itself,' Sotheby's announced in their introduction to the catalog, 'has been untraced since the late 1930s when it was taken out of Austria.'

"Now gee, and duh! What was happening in Austria in the late 1930s? Who can remember? How did it happen to get out of Austria? Sotheby's, who had to know the story, would only say, 'Many different rumours (possibly none of them exactly correct) have suggested its subsequent fate.' Except it turned up on their block and they sold it."

"I missed all that," Fred said. "Where I was in December of 1983, we didn't get news."

Hannah turned the parchment over and began to study the *Hell*. "The *Gospels of Henry the Lion* was a great book, no doubt about it. It's older than this by a couple of hundred years, highly decorated, and of course it belonged to a fabulous guy. But the style is Byzantine. There's no getting around it. Sleepy and square and dull. This is much closer to home.

"God, what I wouldn't give to watch them at Sotheby's, and knock the smug grins off their self-satisfied faces. Listen to how they wrapped up their introduction to the *Henry the Lion* catalog. 'It [the manuscript] has probably had no more than six owners in its 800-year life, but these include a count and a princess, two cathedrals, an emperor, and a king. It will be an expensive book on 6th December. But, unless some revolution overthrows one of the three or four largest national collections, we believe that no greater single manuscript will ever be sold.' Signed, Sotheby & Co. Can you beat them for modest shit-eating vainglory?

"What I have in my hand—the implications that ride on just this sample—historically, artistically, and also commercially—makes the *Gospels of Henry the Lion* look sick.

"To start with, who cares about an artist named Herimann? The Limbourg brothers are not only great, they're known. And they have appeal, the kind of appeal that sells calendars. The Berry *Book of Hours* at Chantilly is reproduced everywhere. Those *Months*—well, hell, you must have recognized *June*, in the *Lazarus* picture. Then there's their Cloisters *Book of Hours* too, which in some ways is not inferior to the big one at Chantilly. In both Books of Hours we know that all three brothers were working: Paul, John, and Herman; and we know what the Duke of Berry paid them after he took them over. We know the duke kidnapped a girl and gave her to Paul as a wife—which you would not do for just anyone—and lots of other good things. And we know that the Duke of Berry and all three of the Limbourg brothers died one after the other in 1416, bang, bang, bang, bang.

"I worked my tail off yesterday on this thing." Hannah flipped the parchment over and studied the *Lazarus* again. "The two Books of Hours I mentioned can be dated between 1406 and 1413..." She turned abruptly and went back to Clayton's chair, crossed her legs, and remarked, "We agreed that Mr. Reed was to give me a check."

"It's my dime," Fred said. He pulled a check from his wallet and filled it out.

Hannah, as she accepted it, gazed at the check with a new speculation that, among other things, reflected the appearance of Fred's car. "I was under the impression," she faltered. "*You* are the principal?"

"I represent the work," Fred said. "Go on with your story."

"Not to get carried away," Hannah continued, "the so-called beautiful and noteworthy Bible the Limbourg brothers started—at least two of them—for Philip the Bold, just disappeared. Vanished. It's not in the record. It's not in the inventory of Philip the Bold's library made after his death. Nobody, but nobody, knows where the Bible went."

Fred strolled to the piano and looked down at the manuscript. "Funny," he said. "I'd assumed, a thing of this quality— especially given today's activity—must be well known, maybe the missing folio 331 from a book in a documented collection that the Germans got from the ruins of Lodz, or Goering bought, using applied duress, from a Belgian collector, or a GI filched from the cathedral treasury in Rheims during the Nazi retreat, or…"

"Elaborate all you want," Hannah interrupted. "There's champions in the art of elaboration in every field. But when your elaboration is built on speculation, you've got nothing but speculation with a lot of frills. Take, for instance, the manuscript in the Bibliothèque Nationale in Paris, which is known to the seven people who care as *Bibl. nat. fr. 166*. It's what's called a *Bible moralisée*. That's a kind of holy comic book they did back then, where most of the story was laid out in pictures, maybe eight to a page, with a scrap of written text to tell you what's going on: maybe an angel showing St. John the Great Whore, or God separating the earth from the heavens.

"There's a gang of scholars—I don't name names, because these folks are in for a surprise: egg-on-the-face big time— that for years have been publishing proof, so they pretend, that this particular *Bible moralisée, fr. 166*, is the very same lost Bible that Paul and John Limbourg made for Philip the Bold between 1402 and 1406. By the way, *nobody* knows where the three boys were after 1404, until they turn up again in 1408, which is the year the Duke of Berry stole that girl, Gilette de Mercier, and gave her to Paul, the eldest.

"Never mind. Here's what we care about. I'm going to concentrate on the *Lazarus*. It's a puzzle. The scholars will have a field day when this gets published. Fred, when you get a chance, look up the reproductions of the *Très Riches Heures* of Jean, duc de Berry. It's a day book, made to assist the private devotions of rich people. Such books varied in kind and content. This one was meant to be used year-round. It included saint's days and prayers and a beautiful full-page image to represent each of the year's twelve months.

"Any library will have copies of the replica edition. Look at *June*. Then look at your *Lazarus*. You'll see when you do, those peasants making hay back of the graveyard are the same peasants, but done ten years earlier for Philip the Bold's bible. When they did the scene for the second time, for the duc de Berry, the Lazarus theme was dropped from the foreground. Instead, where the earlier version had showed nothing but summer sky painted with a week's wages worth of lapis ultramarine—they filled the horizon with the Hotel de Nesle, the Duke of Berry's castle on the bank of the Seine, in Paris. It's where he died, not long after England's Henry V beat the French at Agincourt."

Fred said, "You were suspicious when you saw the *Lazarus*. 'That sarcophagus is familiar,' you said, or 'too familiar.'"

"Well, it is. You get exactly the same image, the same dying Greek of a naked corpse, the same carved coffin a duke could afford but not Lazarus, even half of the same surprised mourners, in the *Lazarus* Herman Limbourg painted for the Duke of Berry's *Book of Hours*. It's folio 171, recto. I'm amazed you didn't recognize it yourself, at least the *June*. It's reproduced everywhere."

"You're working fast," Fred said.

"There'll be thousands of clues to follow when we really start cooking. What plants are those, running around the text? Can we identify the subjects of the portraits of those two clerics being dragged into *Hell* on the other side? Which, by the way, is almost identical to folio 108 recto in the Duke of Berry's *Book of Hours*. While you're there, look at the initial and its decoration, across from the *Lazarus*, where Jesus is baptizing St. John in the Jordan river. That tree is all done in gold leaf, which I can't think of in any other example, and on either side of the tree, holding up the initial, are a white eagle and a white lion."

"That struck me also," Fred said. "Not that I've actually had the time to study this. The animals look heraldic."

"And remember that heraldry is a code, a language," Hannah Bruckmann said. "Language means something. I'm going to find that emblem, though it may take time. How much time do we have?" She had folded Fred's check when he gave it to her, and had been holding it in her right hand while they talked. She ripped it across, and across again, and again, and dropped the fragments onto the silver tray next to her, where Clayton's sherry glass still sat from two nights before.

"All right," Hannah said. "Show me the rest of it."

Chapter 18

"You can't keep this up. The parchment's so smooth, so sweet, so unabraded," Hannah continued, "it can't have been out of its matrix for long—the parent book—which hasn't been seen or heard of for six hundred years.

"Fred, I've been honest with you. I don't know anyone else in the business who'd be this fair. My father, who lived in a different world—and I mean nothing against him—would have offered you twenty-five hundred dollars for that anonymous fragment, not identified it for you as I have and told you its importance. There was no place for trust in my father's world. He'd lost everything under the Nazis, including his parents. He barely got out with his life, and that's all he had. Here, in the States, because he knew books better than anyone except maybe Kraus, he started again and did well. He trusted no one aside from his wife and his daughter.

"I've had better luck. I can afford—not to trust—I'm no fool—but to suspend distrust. I can't appraise the *Limbourg Bible* if I can't see it. I'll tell you right off I can't buy it. I can't afford it. I can sell it, though, which I'd rather do anyway than put a group together to buy it from you for resale. It must be six hundred pages. Couldn't be less. In what—two volumes? Three? You have them all? Of the one you broke apart, you saved the bindings? You didn't—I would have known by now—take other pages elsewhere. You've been canny, I'll say that for you.

"This is a treasure, just the one folio. Yes, it will bring a better price alone than within its book. True, you'll make more by keeping the rest hidden, because if the market learns that the rest exists somewhere, everyone will conspire to keep the page price down.

"My commercial instinct opposes my respect for history, but I'm pleading with you, take the loss. I guess that's what my five thousand dollars is about." She gestured toward the scraps of Fred's check. "Though it means less money, don't sell it in pieces. Keep the book together. It's a whole thing, like a building…"

"Or a person," Fred finished. That stopped her. "With a lot of moving parts. Please stop talking money. You don't know me; it just makes me mad. I don't care about money more than you can imagine. I've been up to my ass in the glory of money all day, from the pretty boys out of the big bright world who wear money and eat it and flaunt it and worship money and call it art. Hannah, if we're going to get along, don't talk money. Pardon me. Or I'll throw you out."

Fred pulled the pillowcase over the parchment and hesitated in the center of the room.

"And when I tell you I don't own this thing," he continued, "don't pretend you know better. Don't call me a liar."

"I want to handle the *Limbourg Bible*," Hannah said.

"Which is another reason to drop me a five thousand dollar tip or bribe," Fred said. "That little piece of theater is supposed to lead to a commission in the high six figures for you, no? Do you have a deal with Marlowe too?"

"It was a clumsy gesture," Hannah said, after a pause. "That's the doorbell. Do you want to see who it is?"

"No," Fred said. "Find us a beer in the kitchen if you have time. I have to make a phone call."

Having unplugged all the telephones on this floor as well as the floor below, Fred connected the nearest one while Hannah Bruckmann found the kitchen. Sam answered and before he could default to Molly, Fred pinned him. "How was it on the river?"

"Aunt Pheely got a new canoe, a Windsong, which sounds more like a sailboat. She says it's the best. It sucks. It tries all the time to go sideways."

"Who was steering?"

"Aunt Pheely. She's heaviest. You always say…"

"Whenever I'm with your Aunt Pheely, we kinda go sideways," Fred said. "You try that Windsong some time when you're steering. See if it doesn't go straight. Put Terry up front. Ophelia made sure you were wearing your life jacket?"

"I'll get Mom," Sam said.

"I've never known him to do it before, but Clayton left a message. Good thing I caught what that rascal Sam had done, and changed it, for the message on my end. Can you imagine? *You have the right to remain silent*…Clay'd still be running. Anyway. Clay actually allowed his voice to be recorded. He said—no, I'll play it for you."

After clicks and subdued female curses, the telephone gave up Clay's voice. "Lady Molly, forgive me. I interrupt a peaceful Sunday. The following recorded communication shall be for Fred. Fred, I am alarmed and dismayed. Five separate people at this gathering have approached me on the *qui vive*, a few quite importunately, seeking access to what appeared in my parlor last Friday evening. I am hounded! This is unlike you. Please be more discreet in future. I say this with all due…" The tape refused to hold more.

"You'll be here tonight?" Molly asked.

"Molly, this business is getting out of hand. There's so many white collar criminals circling in to the scent of what I picked up, I've started to look behind me for the blue collar ones. It's hairy. I'll call you."

"Fred…"

"Soon as I can. This woman's here, the book dealer."

But Molly had hung up. When Fred put the phone down the ring began immediately.

"Sorry, honey, I thought you'd gone," Fred said.

"…will publish a separate hard-cover catalog, fully illustrated, with explanation and notes by our staff or, should you prefer, by distinguished scholars of your selection." The speaking voice was so refined that it was impossible to assign it either a sex or a national origin. Fred let it play on, listening as if he'd walked into a hotel room and found the TV going. "…can still make good room for it as the centerpiece of our December sale, despite the fact that the catalog has gone to press. Due to its great importance, we will reserve the cover for this lot. Our board is prepared to protect your interest by making a substantial guarantee…."

"What are you, for god's sake?" Fred asked. "A recording?"

"…and, it need not be said, our absolute discretion as to the owner's identity," the voice continued. "Payment will be made in the country of your choice, in the currency of your choice. We are prepared…"

"I'll say you're prepared," Fred said, unplugging the telephone's cord again. Hannah, who had been standing in the kitchen doorway holding two bottles of beer by their necks in one hand, and two glasses in the other, was waiting until she understood that Fred was free.

"We'll drink these. Then I'm out of here," Fred said. "Hannah, you have no interest beyond our agreement. I'm writing you a check." He took another from his wallet and started to fill it out. "If anything else develops, we can talk.

"Next, understand that the person who dropped that parchment is truly out of my reach. I can't talk to her or him. I don't even know that it's the property of that person, however the Swiss might see it. I want to know whose it is, that's all. All the rest makes a distracting story I don't need. When I want romance I can find it in a canoe."

He stopped to drink from the bottle, at the same time watching Hannah pouring her beer into one of Clayton's tall glasses. They had both remained standing on one of Clay's rose-colored oriental rugs, as if the rest of the cocktail party had suddenly been sucked, clinking and chattering, into the ovens.

"Whether it's a country or a person or a bank or the cathedral of Quedlinburg, my only interest is to get that thing to where it belongs," Fred said. "I'm working back from where I started. What you do, until my five thousand dollars is used up, start from the other end. It's only been six hundred years. Start with Philip the Bold. Work forward from 1402. Maybe we'll meet in the middle."

"You're so full of advice," Hannah replied, her eyes sparkling with anger. "Get that list we forced out of the Swiss Bankers Association, the names attached to the World War II-era dormant accounts. Try Peter Reber, last heard of in Rhinfelden, Germany. Try Dr. Otokar and Berta Bas, of Prague, Czechoslovakia; Lucie Kroneberg of Yekaterinebourg, Russia; Juro Adleaic of Ljubljana, Slovakia; Anna Trepazonian of Yerevan, Armenia; Sophie Marie Lucie Traca of Bavay, France; Manfred Vogel of Lustenau, Austria. Vogel. Those birds have flown."

Hannah drank the remainder of her beer and wiped her mouth on the back of a hand.

Fred said, "There's such a crowd in front, why don't you leave by the back door? Follow me. I'll call you."

Hannah Bruckmann warned, "There's no way I'll keep this quiet now. As we both know, it's out."

"Clay and I couldn't keep it quiet either. Ben Marlowe spread it around. Them's the breaks." Fred led her down the spiral metal staircase into the office where he kept his desk.

She followed him along the passage between the racks where Clay stored the pictures he wanted to get to easily.

"I'll find a taxi on Charles Street," Hannah said.

Fred locked the door behind her. "Call Molly back," he directed himself, connecting the telephone again, which immediately began to ring.

A sweet female voice began, "…and I have a direct line to Bill Gates. William Gates, of Microsoft, you know, who paid thirty-one million dollars at Christie's for Leonardo's *Codex Hammer*…"

Fred unplugged the phone and climbed the stairs. The voice had been that of the art dealer Lavinia Randall Whitman. He rummaged in the kitchen wastebasket for last Friday's *New York Times*, complete with plastic wrapper, and carried it into the parlor.

Chapter 19

It was again Jackie Banner on watch at the desk in the Chestnut Street vestibule. Fred handed over the blue *New York Times* package, telling him, "Put that in the desk drawer and hold it for me, will you? It's labeled with my name. I get hit by a bus, or take off for Mexico, give it to Molly Riley, along with the cash I've got in the strongbox. Molly can take it from there."

Jackie Banner shoved the package into the bottom drawer and closed it. He asked Fred, "Anything else?"

"Teddy sleeping upstairs?"

"In general. Not right now. He went out."

"I'll be off, then," Fred said.

"Suppose we don't hear from you for some time?" Jackie Banner asked. "At what point do we say you're gone?"

"I didn't mean to be melodramatic," Fred said. "Accidents happen is all I'm thinking. I don't want that package lost."

"You got it," Jackie Banner said and went back to the Danielle Steel he was reading.

⁓

It was eight by the time Fred reached the Lovett Shoe building. He used Jacob Geist's keys and let himself in, climbing the stairs to the fourth floor. It was laid out like the third, with a wide central corridor off of which opened closed doors.

Fred walked the whole length of the building, finding only one doorway that suggested habitation. Next to that door, on the flaking plaster wall, were pinned and taped a number of flyers and posters for exhibitions of photographs by Felice Beamer. Her repeated theme was naked persons wearing veils of gauze or plastic while they reclined or exercised in spiritually nondescript surroundings. From the far side of the door came the Mozart clarinet concerto that tells you to expect the worst when you walk into the dentist's workroom. The smell of frying sausage accompanied Mozart. Fred knocked. The music stopped.

The building was suddenly quiet, except for the distant sounds of sausage objecting to the heat. Fred studied the black-and-white reproductions of Beamer's photographs. They represented seven years of effort, as well as the mutual investment of both artist and small galleries in exhibitions of her work in Lowell, Vineyard Haven, Fall River, Scituate, and Gardner, Massachusetts. The images projected the romanticism of the nineteenth century, although with the late twentieth century's taste for making explicit the facts of life the nineteenth century had felt needed no elaboration. There were solo images of both men and women, as well as images of couples and even groups of three.

"Beamer! I respond to your work!" Fred called.

The thick blue bathrobe in the doorway when it opened did not conceal the woman whose athletic Jacob's Pillow style postures appeared in several of the photographs. In the photos she made the most of a flying mass of kinked black curls, which were now tied up in a red handkerchief of the kind cowboys wear around their necks when they are selling cigarettes. Her round face looked at Fred with speculation. Except that it was higher, the studio space behind her was the size of Jacob Geist's, but largely empty except for tripods and lights and bolts of material, and the king-sized futon on the floor that also appeared in some of the photographs.

"You're perfect," Beamer said. "Also you're early, so you're better than perfect. I can't wait to see the rest of you. How did you get in the building? You locked it behind you?" She made space for Fred in the doorway while she talked by stepping backwards into the studio. She'd covered all her windows with opaque paper. The ceilings in this room were high, twelve feet. It was a huge space, draughty.

"I interrupted your dinner," Fred said. "Yes, I did lock the door."

"You know my work?" Beamer asked, delighted. She crossed her studio space to a cabinet from which she removed both a hot plate and the frying pan. "We're not meant to live here. I figured you were management, trying to catch me," she continued. She retrieved her sausage from a bag under the sink, brushed it off and dropped it into the frying pan. "So you know what I'm looking for," she said. "Seeing you, you make me start thinking ahead. You're as strong as you look? I forgot your name already."

"Fred."

"I'm Beamer. Nobody calls me Felice and lives. I'll eat, then we'll get to work. I don't need you naked today. Richard explained what I'm after…"

"Not really." Fred shook his head. Beamer pulled a slice of soft white bread out of a package and, using it as both potholder and sandwich wrapper, lifted the sausage out of the frying pan and started to eat it, breathing hurriedly around mouthfuls to cool them as she chewed.

"How many are you in this building?" Fred asked.

"The place is condemned and sold. They've got rid of most of us already, but they can't evict us without cause," Beamer explained through her food. "So they can't pull it down." Holding the last bite in one hand, she loosened the belt of her wrapper and shimmied out of it. "Not unless they catch us cooking or sleeping here, and the owner lives in Chicago." While she talked she was peeling off the thin pink sweater she'd been wearing under the robe—all she'd been wearing, aside from the head scarf—which she now began to remove, shaking out her hair.

"Take off your jacket and shirt," she ordered. "I actually don't expect you to appear in the series, not this series. *Free Fall*. Richard explained it to you. He dropped me. I told him, *because you're simply too small*." She was moving briskly around while she talked, plugging in powerful lights and clearing the floor area around the futon.

"Also your shoes. I sleep on that futon," she said. Fred parked his shoes and socks by the chair next to the door and took off his jacket and shirt. "What about the super?" Fred asked. "The super doesn't live in Chicago."

"Hell, the super lives in the building himself, in violation," Beamer said. Her well-disciplined body was in its mid-thirties, somewhat more luscious than the current fashion in female dancers. She moved with natural grace not greatly exaggerated by her nudity. "Calls himself the super," she said, scooping an armload of gauze from the floor, giving it a shake, and beginning to drape it loosely around herself. "Put your watch with your shoes so you don't forget it. If the watch shows, I'm busted. I want to be out of time. It isn't my plan. See, your hands and arms might get in this, big as you are. I set the frame up with Richard, then he dropped me. He can't, the super so-called, or he won't, in the year he's been here, fix the bells or the sinks or the wiring. Sweep the halls? You got to be kidding.

"OK. Here's the idea. Free fall. The camera's field is set so it covers from eight feet up off the ground. The shutter will open after my body trips that electric eye, when I pass across it. Stand on the futon. Throw me into the air, across the electric eye's beam. The camera gets what it gets. I choose what I like. We'll practice, don't worry. Catch me. That's sort of key. Don't drop me, OK? If you have to, make sure I land on the futon, and don't you fall on me."

"What do you go, one fifteen?" Fred asked, looking her over for vulnerable points. If she broke, it was going to change the course of the evening. Beamer leaped into his arms, smelling of sausage, developer, and dusty gauze.

"Not even one-ten," Beamer boasted. "Let's try it."

Fred walked his burden to the futon. Her muscles were resilient, taut under their wrapping. She should be able to take care of herself. "Five weeks I tried to make him fix the sink in my darkroom. Then I decided to hell with it and called a plumber. You have lots of scars." She shivered. "Are they real? They're better than Richard's tattoos. Tattoos are so dating. You look like you've been shot. Cool. So my next month's rent check will be less by the eighty dollars I spent on the plumber. I send the owner the receipt stamped paid, and he works it out with Jake. OK? Toss me."

With surprising lightness she whirled into the air, the white gauze flaring in caught thrusts of energy that snapped and flung back around and against the woman, working the air beneath the ceiling with a confusion of female forces. She made a remarkable spectacle.

"Catch me," Beamer reminded Fred. She'd traveled higher than he had intended, almost hitting the ceiling. Fred caught her, set her on the floor, and the gauze settled onto the pair of them.

"Jake the super," Fred said, "lives below you—I mean, as you say, nobody lives here—his studio's on the third floor."

"Which nobody gets inside," Beamer said, breathing quickly. "That was beautiful. You're perfect. We'll see how it works on film. It's what I wanted to feel like—a beetle tossed in a leaf. I'm excited. I'll get the camera working. Maybe higher if you can. So I stay in range, aim for that spot on the ceiling, see it? that looks like a goat." She fiddled with her camera on its tripod, and with other contraptions, before she draped herself again. "Next we'll try it with Mylar," she decided. "Maybe. I love the idea, but Mylar's so slippery I'm afraid when you go to throw me I'm liable to squirt out of your arms like a watermelon seed. You willing to try?"

"If you are," Fred said. She leaped into his arms.

"Anyone else in the building?" Fred asked.

Chapter 20

"Unless I was going to blow my cover," Fred told Molly, "I had to keep tossing this naked woman for two more hours." He was driving out of Charlestown, trying out avenues of explanation to an invisible Molly who sat next to him, unconvinced, in the suicide seat.

"Maybe another approach is called for, given the current unexplained climate that exists between us," Fred decided. The humorous aspect of the past couple of hours might be lost on the Molly of the last few days. It was already after ten o'clock. There'd been no way to telephone. Fred pulled into a Store 24 parking lot and debated making the call now, but he could be in Arlington in less than half an hour. Molly was like as not already in bed, drowsing in front of a television screen filled with those same English people in those same costumes. Down the hall from her, in her own room, Terry would be reading a book about horses, under the covers with a flashlight. In his room Sam—hard to say about Sam. He'd already stepped into the great solitude of adolescence.

Fred bought a canned sandwich and carried it to the car.

"You brought me a snack," Molly said. She'd been sitting up in the kitchen, working a crossword puzzle from the Sunday paper, which she did not do.

"Tuna fish is all they had," Fred said, surrendering his meal. "We still got beer?"

"In the fridge," Molly told him. Fred pulled out a couple of bottles, opened them and sat across from Molly while she started unwrapping paper.

Fred said, "Once the work week starts again I figure they'll find Jacob Geist's studio first thing, and I lose my clear field. Geist, as I guessed, was living in the Lovett Shoe building, in the studio they let him have in exchange for being the super. The building's owned by a Chicago developer who intends to tear the place down once he gets rid of the tenants. Besides Geist, there's only two tenants left, a photographer named Beamer, and a couple on the top floor, supposed to be paint-ers. I talked to the photographer. The painters weren't there. I'll try them again tomorrow, unless I go to New York. I may go to New York. Sorry, Molly—I didn't mean to stay away so long and then bring work back with me."

"Fred," Molly began and, having his full attention, took a large bite of his sandwich and started chewing it. Fred pulled the puzzle she'd been working on to where he could see how it was going.

"I'm right here," Fred said.

Molly shook her head.

"I couldn't call," Fred explained. "Then by the time I could call, I figured you'd be in bed, maybe asleep."

"We both know you're a free spirit," Molly said. "A free agent as you put it. It doesn't matter."

In a while, "Not to change the subject," Fred answered, "seven down is *rubric*. That c at the end fits into the middle of *projections*."

Molly took another bite and disposed of it before she said, "Jacob Geist was a bomber pilot during World War Two. For their side, obviously."

"Somebody had to do it," Fred said. "How did you find that out?"

"Internet," Molly said.

"Anything else useful?"

"No. It was an article one of the glossies did about the artist after the bicentennial. The *Line of Sweetness*. Short article. Paragraph, actually."

"Teach Sam to use the Internet," Fred said. "It beats the way I work, banging rocks together. Sam and Terry both. Us Neanderthals, maybe we died out for a reason."

Molly shook her head to shut him up.

"No sign of a wife or children?" Fred asked after a while. "In the paragraph?"

Molly's head continued shaking while she crumpled the paper and tossed the ball it made into the air to catch it a few times.

"The parchment's attracting so much activity in the world outside, it turns out it's a big deal," Fred said. "A big enough deal it would justify, for a sorry lot of our fellow humans, killing a person." He took the wad of business cards from his pocket and fanned them to show Molly. "That's just a sample of who stopped by Mountjoy Street. Other people were calling. It's why I unplugged Clay's phones. Tomorrow, now Sunday's over, the day of rest, it's going to start in earnest. Just so you know, I took the thing out of Clay's house and stashed it at Chestnut Street, just in case. Until I can figure out what the devil to do with it."

"What do you mean, Just in case?"

"I mean Just in case," Fred said. "No more no less. It's an open hypothesis. I don't mean to suggest a goddamned thing."

"After you say Geist could have been killed…"

Fred said, "Don't jump to conclusions. For…"

"You can't turn off the ringer?" Molly asked.

"The what?"

"On Clay's phones. Since you don't want to know when people call."

Fred said, "Can you do that?"

They sat in silence with the crossword puzzle between them until, "I don't know what went wrong," Fred volunteered finally. "I'm supposed to guess. I don't have a clue."

"Maybe we should go up and make love, or something like that," Molly suggested.

New York City was filled with rain, which had begun not long after Fred's plane lifted itself out of Logan. Just ahead of a wet pair of cops, Fred bought an umbrella from a sidewalk entrepreneur and used it to parry the other umbrellas on his way to 57th Street. He'd taken an early shuttle. It was not even nine o'clock when he reached the building's double glass doors. He was obliged to make a commotion before the uniformed guard would acknowledge his presence, dismount from his chair, and open the doors wide enough to say, "The building opens at ten."

"Ring Armand Kordero. Tell him I want to see him. Tell him Geist. Jacob Geist."

"Mr. Kordero didn't tell me to expect a guest," the guard objected.

"Give him the message. I'll wait in the rain. He'll like that, having me wait in the rain."

The guard looked doubtful, scratched an armpit of his red uniform with gold buttons and braid on it, and motioned Fred to come in. Fred dripped by the elevator doors while the guard made reverent sounds into his desk telephone.

"He'll talk to you," the guard said, holding out the receiver.

"It's Fred," Fred said. "I got to thinking and I came back."

"You did," Armand Kordero's voice agreed.

"I'm closer to Jacob Geist; but I'm confused."

"Penthouse. I'll instruct the doorman. Pass him to me," Kordero ordered. Fred stood by the elevator doors for about ten minutes until the guard told him, "It stops on ten. Ring the bell next to that keyhole on the wall next to the sign

PENTHOUSE. Mr. Kordero buzzes you up the last floor. He controls it from his end. I can't get you up there."

The elevator doors opened directly into the midst of Kordero's love nest of luxury. Kordero in a pink satin gown, his hair already glued in place, was by himself enough to astound. But the opulent room he stood in—if Louis XIV's servant-girl mistress had spent five years reading movie magazines before Louis told her, "Take this blank check. Make yourself a place where I can attend to you without being ashamed I'm there"—she could not have done more.

"The surrey with the fringe on top," Fred remarked, walking past Kordero and into his cynical decorator's dream of dreams. The place was awash in whipped cream. Everything in it was gilded and plushed and flocked and farced and crusted, embroidered, or at least polished.

Kordero dismissed the compliment with a gesture. "I am drinking tea by the window," he said. He allowed Fred to follow him through a minefield of ormolued bric-a-brac to a fragile table where a teapot sat next to two cups and two bulging pastries. The rain drooled enviously against the outside of the window, and slobbered downward on its panes.

As he sat, Fred glanced quickly around the walls. "Don't see any manhole covers up here," he observed. "No fanny prints by U. Gandrud. What about *Piddle of Pride* number six ninety three by Humbly Benighted? Who did this place over for you? The Limbourg brothers?"

Kordero's gaze remained firm and secretive, wincing steadily through the steam he pretended was rising out of the cup he was drinking from.

"I've seen everything in your inventory with Geist's name on it, between JG-20 and JG-70. Fifty drawings," Fred said. "Fifty *Geistmaps*. You gave me to understand you had them. They are not in the same league as the pretentious, empty shit I saw downstairs."

Kordero put down his rose-colored cup with gilded fribbles. "Where is Jacob Geist?" he asked.

Fred said, "Ah, well."

"Try not to break anything this time, Shep," Kordero said to the wide-shouldered fellow Fred had last seen on Chestnut Street in Charlestown. In a blue suit too tight across the shoulders, Shep, formerly known as John Travolta, stepped from behind the fat swag of pulsing curtain made of red damask with a pattern of golden hemorrhoids.

"Don't move," Shep told Fred.

Chapter 21

The man he'd called Shep stood behind Kordero, menacing, protective, comfortable on his home ground.

"I shall withdraw," Kordero said. "Business. Shep, when you are through, I have questions for the gentleman. If there is to be blood, take him to the game room. Remember..." he finished, standing, and gesturing toward the collection of gaudy fragility in the room. He clutched the pink satin robe tighter around him.

Fred said, "I was asking about the Limbourg brothers when we were interrupted." Kordero inclined his head toward Shep. Fred kept his eyes on the large man in blue while Kordero moved from his field of vision. Shep grinned, rubbing his hands, a couple of paces away, until a door snicked softly closed.

"The most quiet and simple way to get this done," Shep said, "and the easiest way on the furniture, is for you, Fred, to stretch your leg out—I don't care which leg, you choose—so your foot rests on Mr. Kordero's chair. Then I stamp on your knee and break it. After that, when you start to answer Mr. Kordero's questions, he's more prone to believe you."

"I do want to hear Kordero's questions," Fred said. "Don't think I don't."

"Which leg, then?" Shep asked. "No, don't get up." He leaned closer, keeping his distance, maintaining for himself room enough to move quickly in response to whatever adjustment Fred tried. Fred scratched his face. Shep hunched into a speedy crouch, ready to rush, but keeping the table between them.

Fred said, "Then what do you do, drive me home? You think that transmission will make it?"

"The guy wants to talk cars," Shep said. "He does not appreciate the seriousness of his position. We do it the hard way."

His attack was canny, consisting of mixed signals that suggested both western brawl and eastern discipline. Because the head wants to claim all the body's protection at such a moment, he let it seem that his aim was the head, making a show of striking with both his hands, while his right heel kicked for a stunning blow to the chest to knock Fred off balance and backward.

The next instant Shep found his striking foot clamped in Fred's hands. Fred lifted and twisted so fast there was barely time for a look of baffled surprise before Shep tried a whirl to escape. He'd left it a half second too long. Fred held the foot firm, standing slowly and lifting it higher in the exaggerated move of the dance called Charleston. Fred had placed his right foot on Shep's left and bore down as he lifted and twisted, hearing tendons snap and Shep's groan of surprise and pain turning into a wheeze of agony. Fred continued lifting and twisting. He'd gotten the foot so high, and the leg so bent, Shep could no longer support the weight of his upper body, but was forced to struggle to keep balance while he reached to get purchase against his opponent with his hands. His flailing increased the speed of his dislocation. Tea cups chattered. Fred got his shoulder under the knee, bent the lower leg over it; lifted and twisted.

"Oh, Jesus," Shep groaned. The shock of massive sudden pain to the joints of hips, knees, ankles—his whole lower body—made him gasp. There was no luxury room in his lungs for the screams he wanted. Fred gritted his teeth, twisted and lifted. The man was strong, and heavy, and truly unhappy. "You're killing me," Shep told Fred, between hacking attempts at breathing. Tears burst from his eyes. He puked, and his bowels opened. Fred lifted and twisted.

The hip joint gave up first, then the knee; but the ankle held. By the time Fred released and dropped him, Shep was not conscious. "It's a good anesthetic, pain," Fred remarked. "And wonderfully cheap."

The man with the interesting leg lay on a blue Chinese carpet whose prevailing color almost matched his suit. Fred looked around the room cluttered with grandeur. There was no sign of Kordero.

"I can't gag the son of a bitch," Fred worried. "He'll suffocate if he pukes again. But when he wakes up he's going to be noisy."

He tore the golden rope from the curtain and tied Shep's arms and wrists together, anchoring them, for good measure, to the distorted leg. Then he wrapped the man's head in the thick red cloth of the curtain, making a large, loose bundle of it that would muffle whatever Shep had to say. As a final thought, he took the other curtain from the window and draped it across the package he had made.

There were doors off two sides of this room that were not occupied with windows; and on the fourth side, in the direction Kordero had gone, a kitchenette was visible, with passage doors on either side. The one on the right was open, and led to a space more in keeping with the art Kordero sold downstairs. It was a bare room with white tiled floors and walls. Orange stuffed plastic mats lay on the floor, not far from the hanging weight bag, and a few machines. A large shower stall occupied one corner; a director's chair in yellow canvas another. "Game room," said Fred.

The muffled regular moaning came not from Shep—Fred checked—but from back of the other door. Fred eased it open into a grandiloquent bedroom in white and gold, almost Napoleonic in its flavor—Empire, it would be called—complete with the seething billow of Kordero's pink satin robe in the midst of the white circular bed. Kordero's feet in gold slippers protruded from the heave in Fred's direction. The moans came from beneath the satin hump.

Fred grabbed the feet and jerked Kordero toward him, giving a quick flip so he'd fall to the floor face up. His hair flapped backwards like a plate, and lay on the golden rug.

"Shep!" squealed a female voice from the slim pink scrambling body that righted itself and struggled to yank a creamy garment far enough down to cover her own gold fringe with its gold lace border.

"I forget your name," Fred told the woman, at the same time putting a foot firmly on Kordero's stomach. The man had fallen in such a way that his pink robe winged around him. His flab, and his mangy parts, twitched haphazardly while they did their best to shrivel into oblivion. "Something like Muriel," Fred guessed. "Am I close?"

"Mirelle," she said. Kordero grunted under Fred's foot. Mirelle gathered herself together, seeking more cover than the sole garment she wore had been made for.

"Violence. That turns the old boy on," Fred said. "Knowing it's in the next room stiffens old winkie? Stay there a minute, Mirelle. I'm trying to think. You are not going to enjoy what I am about to do to your friend Kordero."

"Try me," Mirelle said, her eyes bright. She licked her lips and dropped the pretense of looking for cover. Fred increased his pressure on Kordero's stomach, and was rewarded with a gasp.

"I can help," Mirelle offered. "Where's Shep?"

Fred said, "I can't ask you to leave."

"Really, I don't mind watching," Mirelle said eagerly. "Whatever you boys want to do. Tell him, Armand. I'm a big girl."

"Shut up," Kordero said.

"That a bathroom?" Fred asked, motioning toward a door on the far side of the room.

"Closet," Mirelle said, shaking her head.

"Tell you what. Get in and stay put," Fred said. "Or, no. We don't know what's in there. That other door. That's the bathroom?" Mirelle nodded. "Wait for me in there," Fred said.

Mirelle clambered off the bed. "Stay where you are," Fred told Kordero, following Mirelle the few steps to the bathroom door. Those were old burn and new bite marks on her buttocks and thighs. She liked pain, or someone did. He looked past her into the gorgeous blue and white bathroom. "Give me that telephone, turn on the water in tub and basin, loud, and keep the door closed until we're ready for you," Fred ordered. Mirelle put a huge white towel around her shoulders and sat on the edge of the tub, reaching for an *Allure* magazine that lay on the floor. Fred closed her in.

"Fred, I don't know," Kordero started. Fred stepped on his plate of hair. The man's little face stared up, pleading.

"The Limbourg brothers," Fred said. "Groucho and Chico and Harpo Limbourg and—I don't know—maybe Zeppo got into the act as well."

"My hair," Kordero begged.

"Your hair's a lost cause," Fred promised. "I'm trying to decide about your head."

"I told Shep to scare you, that's all," Kordero said. "I don't know these Limbourgs."

"Talk to me about what Jacob Geist was carrying for you," Fred said. "Which—so you don't lose more sleep over it—I have."

Kordero's face was blank of any rational element other than fear.

"Whose is it?" Fred demanded.

Kordero tried to shake his head, but the tension of Fred's foot against his remaining pride prevented it.

"Let's try it this way," Fred suggested. Keeping his foot in place, he sat on the edge of the bed and rubbed his arms. "Pretend Shep is through with me, you're through with Mirelle, it's all gone swell this time, you're finished, she's happy, and all the time you've been enjoying the sound of my discomfort from the next room. Maybe Shep joins you and adds whatever grace note he contributes to the loving concert. You mop up, finish your tea, and come scampering into the game room. There I am, eager and ready to answer questions. How am I doing?"

Kordero mumbled, "There was no plan to hurt you in any way. I swear."

"Point noted," Fred said. "Now, still pretending—you sit in your bright yellow director's chair, right? Mirelle's going to do what she likes to do—watch? Or does she help ask questions? Shep's there for the big stuff.

"Pretending all this, my question to you, Kordero, is: what are your questions?"

Chapter 22

"That son of a bitch ran off with my property," Kordero said. He worked to ease the tension on the roots of his masquerade by raising his chin. He noticed next that he was uncovered, and he brought the pink flaps of his robe across his body. "You are standing on my hair," he complained.

"That son of a bitch ran off with my property," Fred repeated. "Go on. What's your question?"

"Where the fuck is Jacob Geist? You found him? Fine. Sell him to me."

"Sell him to you," Fred said.

"You'll get nowhere yourself," Kordero spluttered. "You're crazy. Nobody else in the world can market that junk but me." He moved his chin higher, struggling to arch his back enough to relieve the strain on his hair. "The market's impossibly soft. Where can you go with it?"

Fred exploded, "You call this a soft market?" He could have sold the parchment ten times just yesterday, to people he'd never heard of, who had come looking for him.

"I sold a grand total of three during the show," Kordero whined. "One I had to practically give away. Since we're talking business, why not do it like gentlemen? You have what I want. I'll pay for it, within reason. Let's talk in my office, downstairs. I keep cash there. But I won't go high. I already own everything Geist ever made."

"We're talking about Jacob Geist's pictures?"

"What the fuck do you think we're talking about? His pictures, his body, his life—the works. I own it. What he did in the past, and everything he does in the future."

Fred stepped off the flap of discouraged hair and motioned Kordero to stand if he wanted to. In the bathroom the water roared. Kordero rolled to his front and heaved himself to his feet, tying the sash of the robe and breathing hard, purple with humiliation.

"You can come out," Fred called into the bathroom. Mirelle, wrapped in the towel, edged into the room, using a thumb to hold her place in *Allure*. "Go on down. Open the store," Fred said.

"Like hell. You're fired," Kordero fumed. "I give you two minutes. Get dressed and get out." Kordero marched out of the bedroom, Fred sticking with him. The door slammed after them. Kordero slowed to walk through his cluttered living room showplace, toward the place in the streaming window where his tea had been interrupted. He gazed down at the stinking damask pile when he reached it, then glanced at Fred.

He smiled. "This changes everything," he said. "I made no arrangements for disposal. If we come to an agreement, I'll do what I can for you within reason, but frankly, Fred, as far as my putting money toward anything you can give me, all bets are off.

"Here's the new deal. You give me Geist. I do what I can to keep you clear of this thing." He kicked at the damask pile and got a sick groan. "Oh," Kordero said.

"Geist stole his own work from you?" Fred asked. He took Kordero's elbow and steered him to a love seat in blue satin, squatting in front of the man.

"I own Geist," Kordero said. "I can show you the contract, in my gallery safe. I financed all his works for the past two decades, more. Who do you think paid for his *Line of Fat*?

Whose money financed his *Frontier of Galactic Starlight*, from one end to the other of the Atlantic Ocean? Pole to fucking pole. Who paid for everything since I signed him on, paper included? Two hundred and eighty thousand dollars I've sunk in that man's projects, and only because I believed in what I could make him over the long term. And, frankly, once he's dead. The son of a bitch won't die. You want to earn some honest money? We can talk about that.

"When his show was coming down, Geist pulled a fast one. How he got to her I don't know, but the girl who worked for me at the time—overnight the bastard disappeared. Cleaned out his studio, and took everything with him. Including what I had of his in the gallery. It's all mine. If I find you with any of it, I sue you. When I find *him* I sue. Breach of contract. Breach of fiduciary obligation. Breach of whatever. Nobody welshes on Armand Kordero. That includes the Tibet stuff. He's out of his mind if he thinks I'll finance that, I told him; but that doesn't change the deal: he makes it, I own it. Even a goddamned geek like him can understand that.

"Before we go down to the gallery, drag Shep to his room. I feel faint. My heart." He wrinkled his nose.

"You and Shep work something out," Fred decided, standing as Mirelle, in a slinky tan suit, and carrying a fat overnight bag, emerged from the bedroom.

"Asshole," she told Kordero. "I put your precious suits in the bathtub, and the rest of your clothes. I love that big tub! I'll miss it. Don't bother to count your crap. I took a few things to sell."

She stalked to the elevator and inserted a gold key in the keyhole. "Fred, do me a favor," she continued. "Keep that asshole where he is till it comes. Then, if you're through here, maybe you want to ride down with me? This is the only key. He won't even let Shep have one." She stood by the door, waiting. "And don't give me any trouble, hairless asshole

Armand faggot Kordero," she went on. "Or I'll tell. Don't think I won't. I've got photos, dates, receipts: everything."

"Fred, my best offer is ten thousand dollars," Kordero told Fred as the elevator door opened.

"Shep's going to need help," Fred told him. He joined Mirelle in the elevator, Kordero running toward them as the door slid closed.

"The key! Leave me the key!" he called after them down the shaft. Mirelle tucked it into her purse.

"I'm going to fuck you blind," Mirelle said. She was seething with rage, or merely with opportunity. "We'll stop at the gallery." She'd punched the lobby button already but, as she spoke, she pushed Three.

Fred shook his head. "Kordero's got nothing I want," he said. The elevator descended past Seven and Six.

"Except money," Mirelle said. "Which I will help you get our share of, that bastard. He offers you ten? It means he's got a budget of two hundred thousand. So we demand three. For whatever you have. Then, for the big score...while he sends Shep after Geist... see, the other stuff I think Kordero's into, which I can prove everything, I just need a good man...."

The elevator stopped on Three and the doors opened. Mirelle pressed hold. "He'll change the locks soon as he can. Now's your chance if there's anything you can use. Tell you what. We'll go in his office and fuck. On his desk? In front of his great big window? Would you like that, Fred? You've seen what I've got. It'll take him hours to get out of that penthouse. Locksmith, electrician, who knows, cops? We should of pulled out his phone. What happened to Shep, anyway? What do you say? Live dangerously. You on?"

Fred said, "Kordero's got nothing I want. Neither do you."

"I'm in the book if you change your mind. Mirelle Crowsette. In the book. It's a French name. I made it up."

They rode the rest of the way down in silence until, "Rats," Fred said. "I forgot my umbrella upstairs."

The train to New Haven took a generous hour, but that was long enough for the rain to decrease to a thin piddle, and for Fred to dry out somewhat. The desk at the Royal Court Hotel, New Haven, passed Fred the word that Clayton was lunching in the Parliament Pub and Grill Room, and would be glad of his company. The hotel's lobby was decorated with English hunting prints and themes, with mounted fox heads and racks of fossil horns from Irish elk. Fred followed the Pub signs until he arrived at the clicking rattle of a fake British pub, complete in every detail except for the reek of smoke and the sense that anyone belonged here.

Clay, with Lakshmi Thomas nowhere visible, was seated against the wall, on a bench, under a mullioned window stained the color of ale. In place of Lakshmi he faced a man with protuberant ears and a back ruff of white hair under a dome of wrinkled skin. Seeing Fred enter, Clay tried to get up, though the table prevented him. His companion, caught up in the flow of action, pushed his chair back and, turning, rose.

"Fred Taylor is joining us," Clay said, his hunted eyes filled with relief. "Fred, may I introduce Doctor Galéas Visconti Valentine?"

Fred took the clean hand that was offered along with the doctor's claim, "*Enchanté*," in an Italian accent.

"Disregard the menu," Clay advised. Fred dragged a heavy chair over and sat next to Dr. Valentine. "I made the mistake of ordering Bubble and Squeak. It is not up to British standards. Doctor Valentine, more fortunate, chose the Ploughman's Lunch. Though far from authentic, one can at least divine what the ingredients are meant to be.

"Doctor Valentine holds the Boucicaut Chair of Medieval Studies, Fred. He has been explaining to me that though his primary affiliation is academic, he nonetheless professes a confidential relationship with the Hesdin Library, as well as being a curator for the Colombe Rare Book Room at Yale.

He has been explaining—Doctor Valentine, would you care to repeat for my colleague's ears what you have already suggested to me?"

"I'll have a hamburger," Fred told the buxom serving wench who looked ready to burst with the indignity of her costume. "With fries. I'll call it whatever I have to. A London Bridge? That's what I want, a hamburger. Can you manage that?"

"If I have to make it myself," she said.

Dr. Valentine forked bean sprouts onto an olive and speared a tomato slice with the arrangement. He held the forkful in the air while he looked dubiously from Fred to Clayton and back again.

"Fred enjoys my fullest confidence," Clay assured him.

"Very well. On behalf of the Hesdin Library," Dr. Valentine began...

"You have authority to represent the Hesdin Library?" Fred asked.

Valentine colored. "These are subtle matters. The area of mutual interest served by both academe and an institution such as the Hesdin—oftimes these areas overlap and become indistinguishable, one from another. Each of us must serve many masters. My own expertise...."

"I get it. Valentine is another of the crowd of jokers that's trying to get next to that blessed Bible?" Fred asked Clay.

Clay's shrug acknowledged an affirmative.

"Then I can save us all time. I got rid of the blasted thing this morning," Fred announced.

Dr. Valentine dropped his fork with a crash. The slice of tomato, with its comet tail of sprouts, sailed toward the next table. Clay's mouth had dropped open before he snapped it shut.

Chapter 23

Dr. Galéas Visconti Valentine did not recall his previous engagement right away. He tried to wheedle out of Fred, or Clay, or both, any hint of where the Bible had gone, not knowing, or not mentioning at least, the Limbourg participation in it. Fred and Clay rested mute. As Valentine's dismay increased, only exacerbated by Fred's attention to his hamburger when it came, his English became worse, falling more and more victim to a murderously quick Italian accent.

"It is sold?" Valentine demanded. "Or is it merely in the hands of a broker? What broker? Kraus? Sam Fogg?"

"Sam Fogg's a dealer?" Fred asked.

"My client demands first refusal," Valentine said.

Fred asked, "Which client? The Colombe Rare Book Room, your employer, or the heap of old pirate treasure that's being recycled through the Hesdin Library?"

"At least say what country it's in," Valentine pleaded.

Fred dipped a fry in ketchup and used it to accentuate a question. "Suppose we know that the work in question was stolen, let's say during the past war?"

Clay intruded over Valentine's gesture of reassurance, "Dr. Valentine assures me that this has seldom been an impediment in the past. In the case of Yale, perhaps—though were the work to be sold to a potential donor to Yale, that might obviate—but in any case, as far as Dr. Valentine is concerned,

Yale is out of the question. He prefers to work with the Hesdin Library. The Hesdin has no such compunctions…"

"Tell you what," Fred told Valentine. "If I have something to say, I'll call you. Now it's time for you to suddenly recall a previous engagement."

"I shall report that man to my alma mater," Clay fussed once Valentine had departed. "I am in torment. I cannot abide that my business be known to all and sundry. I shall join a monastery. The idea of that two-faced jackal. Another gold-digging academic. I am outraged. His allegiance should be purely to Yale. It was a subtle ruse, your telling him the piece had been disposed of. It *was* a ruse?"

"A ruse, yes. Though it is no less out of reach."

"I have been thinking, Fred. I may have been impetuous earlier. I do acknowledge that the matter is entirely yours to decide. You must be a free agent, I see that. Still, when the subject's ownership and provenance are understood, Fred, I know I may rely on you…"

"It's out of your reach," Fred said, gathering the remaining fragments of his meal into a final bite. The lunch crowd had thinned while they were talking with Valentine. They were far enough from their nearest neighbor to converse comfortably.

Fred had ordered coffee. Clay professed to avoid stimulants, and was sipping from a cup of hot water, "to settle my nerves. I am badgered unceasingly. Those who are not seeking to buy from me what I do not yet own, are asking to sell it. Or they solicit it, sight unseen—indeed nobody specifies exactly what they believe the object is—as a keystone gift for whatever important collection, which is also by coincidence seeking trustees. Hautschild flew in from Zurich, he avers, specifically to importune me, and I received this morning an engraved fax from Tanneguy du Châtel, regretting that he happens to be in Venice. He offers to pay my way should I incline to visit him there. With, he implies, a package under my arm.

"Worse, seeking to press an assault on the distaff side, attempts have been made to suborn Ms. Thomas."

Was that an unaccustomed tremble in Clay's voice? An unusual pallor visiting his cheek? He soldiered on. "She has behaved very well. Very well indeed. Several men have attempted crassly to buy information from her. Another is, even as we speak, escorting her to luncheon in the Crystal Palace. I instructed Ms. Thomas to learn what she could from this gentleman."

"You're sure that's wise?" Fred asked.

"She knows nothing. Thus she can reveal nothing," Clayton said. "Consequently I have every confidence in her. Every confidence. Thank God we are alone, Fred, given your adroit finesse of Dr. Valentine's interference. He thrust himself on me. Your being in New Haven unexpectedly shows that you have made progress. Whom must I pay for the parchment? How much? I'm frantic with expectation. Is it true that you have discovered an entire bible? We shall talk in my room."

Fred threw enough money on the table to cover his meal, with tip. "Clay, I stopped in with the simple Dickensian message: don't go home. Your place is surrounded. Bad as it is here, you might as well stay on for a while. I don't know what's coming next. The parchment's as hot as it looks."

"Developments?" Clay asked.

"Yes, though I'm no closer to understanding the situation than I was last Friday when I took that thing out of the air."

Clay's face puckered in consternation. "The rain has stopped. Let us walk the streets of New Haven. Incidentally, I apologize for Benjamin Marlowe. This is his fault, this stampede, as you said. I did reach him last night by telephone. His inexcusable interference in my affairs, he said, was based on his desire to assist."

"It is *my* affair," Fred said. "Marlowe blabbed because he smelled a commission. We both know that."

Clay pocketed the money Fred had dropped and handed the serving wench his gold card. "The wretch Valentine leaves me to pay his bill. Never mind. This entire sojourn in New Haven is either business or charity. I have not yet decided which. In either case, it is the government who shall pay."

***

The streets of New Haven, even washed and refreshed, as on an afternoon in October with the leaves turning, still resemble, a tired old sailor who's been rolled for his money, left in the gutter, and rained on. Fred and Clayton walked the short distance to the Yale campus and plunged into its oasis of wishful thinking. Knots of students crossed their path, their eyes on meaningful lives in other places, soon, for which their brief New Haven exile was to prepare them.

Fred told Clay, "I took the manuscript out of your house. Whether it is Jacob Geist's heirs, or someone else, I haven't located the owner. While the ownership question's pending, I won't tease you with Hannah Bruckmann's preliminary opinion except to let you know that she guesses a value of a million dollars."

Clay's face went gray. "Great Heavens! No wonder..." he yelped.

"For the single folio sheet," Fred went on, relentless. Clay tottered. Fred guided him to a bench. After a few moments, "I had no idea. But perhaps the owner is not aware..." Clay hazarded.

"Ah, but *I* am," Fred said. "Whoever the owner is, until and unless I am satisfied, I represent that owner. For now all I know is that the owner has expressed no interest in selling. Furthermore, it's worth more than you'd pay. If it's part of an extant book or books—which everyone seems, on the basis of no evidence whatsoever, blithely to assume—your interest is even less. A book like that would be worth more than the Beineke."

"I never dreamed," Clay said, stunned. The enormity of his loss danced under the sad wet leaves that flopped from the trees of Yale. He stared at the cruelty of the dance's impossible seduction. "Perhaps there is another way to look at this. Should one speak in terms of mere monetary value," Clay said finally, "one would be obliged to factor in this consideration. Fred, in your cynical way, you are fond of saying that art is used as currency. Within limits you are correct.

"With this caveat. Art corresponds only to *expendable* currency. Leonardo's *Leicester Codex*—I refuse to refer to it as the *Codex Hammer*—that upstart!—was able to sell for thirty million only because Gates had thirty million in cash he could do *without*, and his underbidder believed he was able to live equally happily without twenty-nine million. They didn't have to eat that money, as you would say. They didn't even need to invest it. They could, essentially, burn it.

"To buy such an object is not like putting down cash for a company such as Hormel Ham or General Motors. My point is, the concept of *expendable* currency has stricter limitations. Perhaps…"

"My train's at four," Fred said. "Unless you want to help me, I guess you are out of this now, Clay. I wanted to be sure you understood. We've always acknowledged that such an occasion might arise, and it has arisen. True, you are being inconvenienced over my business. But that is on account of Ben Marlowe, whom you brought into this. I'll try to keep you informed of my movements until I get this settled, as far as it makes sense. I want to tell Lakshmi to keep her head down. And, as I say, you might be less badgered here than you would be at home."

Clay said, "The note in my box, telling me to expect a visit from the Belgian ambassador—your counsel is to avoid her?"

"Absolutely. For all we know, Belgium guesses this thing was taken by force from one of its citizens, and therefore the government feels it can make its own claim for possession.

To continue. If I can learn from Molly's contacts where Geist's passport shows he'd been before he met the grim reaper in terminal E, I may even leave for Europe either tonight or tomorrow morning. I don't know. We'll adjust my salary as needed. As of this moment, and until further notice, I'm not working for you."

"You are working against me," Clay agreed.

"Independent of you," Fred said. "I've got to go. In this case what you want isn't germane to what I've got, that's all. I'll get this taken care of as soon as I can."

The revolving Crystal Palace, on the roof of the Royal Court Hotel, provided far too much view of the belated hopes of New Haven. At a groaning board down the center of the empty restaurant, grown men dressed as Beefeaters, hairy bearskin busbies and all, stood ready to carve from joints of beef, ham, lamb, or from suckling pigs, turkeys, geese, ducks, capons.

Lakshmi Thomas, a radiance of white lace and tawny skin, was sipping green liquid from a crystal goblet, across from a keen young man with a keen young face and a keen young haircut, who leaned across the table toward his companion and whispered urgently. When Fred put a hand on the shoulder of his blue blazer, the man jumped.

"Here you are," Fred said.

Chapter 24

"Fred, you scare people," Lakshmi Thomas complained. The young man had half stood. The weight of Fred's hand prevented his rising higher.

Pulling a chair to the table, Fred asked, "May I join you?"

"Excuse my ugly friend," Lakshmi told the young man. The gold necktie on him was covered with black beetles. "His name is Fred. I can't keep him from defending me. Fred, Andrew Beach is my lover. We are making love."

"Oops!" Fred said.

"Andrew teaches Physics at Yale," Lakshmi explained. "Therefore I kill two birds…"

"Clay thought you were being hit on by another manuscript salesman. Sorry." Fred took Andrew's hand briefly and stood again.

"I sell only photons," Andrew Beach said.

"I'll leave you to it. The weekend went OK?" Fred asked Lakshmi.

"Too many speeches. Too many olives. Too many old men with nothing to do. Mr. Reed is a sweetie, but when it is time for small talk he complains about Thomas Pynchon. From the way he talks, I believe Mr. Reed has been holding the book upside down."

"May we speak confidentially in front of Andrew?" Fred asked.

"We are lovers, Andrew and I," Lakshmi said. "Is it more confidential than that, what you have to say?"

"I want the names of the people who tried to buy information from you."

"Sure." Lakshmi put down her goblet and riffled through her purse, took out three business cards and, with a blinding smile, handed them over. "On each card I write how much the person will pay me to betray Mr. Reed. I smile and say I will think about it."

Fred tucked the cards in his shirt pocket. "Sorry I interrupted."

———

By six o'clock Molly should be home, with dinner prepared for the children. Fred was still over an hour south and west of Boston, eating train peanuts and drinking train beer. He got hold of the train's telephone and caused it to reach Molly.

"I'm just the wrong side of Providence," Fred told her.

"Terry, get out of here until it's ready," Molly screeched. "Fred? Dee left a message for you. That license number you gave her? MA 193–123 is a white Ford Taurus wagon, belongs to Rent-a-Wreck, the one out by Logan Airport. Dee says if you want her to find out who rented it, tell her what date and time. The person driving it today is a priest, Father Myron Nutting, from Charlotte, North Carolina....No, Terry, I told you already a thousand times. Get lost. I'm on the phone. When I'm not talking it means I'm listening. When I am talking, it means I don't want to listen to you."

Three large college-aged women struggled past Fred carrying the train's cardboard box trays overflowing with cans, chips, ice, nuts, fruit. They stepped on his feet and spilled things on him, laughing and joking amongst themselves while they picked them up and made a fuss of apology.

"Don't worry about Lakshmi," Fred said. "If Clay has designs on her, they miss her by a mile. She's got an appropriate someone to love in New Haven. She accepted Clay's ride, is all, to come and see him. I met him. You'd approve."

"Isn't Lakshmi a free agent?" Molly asked. "Wasn't that what you kept saying? Fred, I'm rushed."

Fred asked, "Just quickly, did you get a chance to talk to Dee's friend's friend again? About where Geist had been, or what they think happened to him?"

"I work all day," Molly answered. "I've got Terry's school's open house in an hour. You're coming back to Arlington tonight?"

"I'll make a stop in Charlestown. If you think of it, leave me the name and number of Dee's friend's friend."

"I can't talk now," Molly said.

A fat man with large suitcases and larger adenoids forced his way past. The connection was gone once the commotion cleared.

"It's impossible they haven't tracked him yet," Fred exclaimed, sitting in his car far enough along Arnold Street to maintain an unobtrusive surveillance on the Lovett Shoe building. He'd been watching for twenty minutes. "I'll tell Sam there's a future job for him—doing detective work on the Internet for the police or State Department." Nothing had gone into or come out of the building.

He prowled through the parking lot and looked up at the back. No light shone on the third floor, where someone official should be showing an interest in Jacob Geist's relicts. No light shone on the fourth floor, where Felice Beamer's windows were blacked out anyway. Only the fifth floor showed light, in two adjacent rooms.

A good deal of traffic, both vehicle and foot, was out this Monday evening. Arnold was the preferred route to use for those wanting to get somewhere other than Arnold Street.

Fred went back to his car. "You let me down, Molly," Fred said, watching the street. "The only way to get past futile imagining is with fact. I don't even know what the man died of. Given that ruthless bastard Kordero; given the washable playroom and torture chamber he keeps for his gimpy buddy Shep—given the stink of money and intrigue we've stirred up since last Friday—how can I not suspect that Jacob was killed? How can I not assume that the parchment is evidence in a crime bigger than smuggling? A crime with blood and hopeless grief in it—generations of grief?

"After Hannah Bruckmann's hints, how can I not think Auschwitz, Dachau, Babi Yar?"

A flock of gulls screamed out of the Navy Yard, circled the Lovett Shoe building, gave up, and decided to stick with the Navy Yard.

"Where were we?" Fred asked himself. "Yes. Fifth floor. Katz/Moncrieff. Where there's light, there's hope."

He went straight to the top floor. Here most of the doors to the rooms leading off the central hallway had been removed from their hinges and carried away. "Jacob's drafting tables," Fred recalled, nodding as he walked along. Without its connecting doors, this floor had slid more precipitously toward the building's impending ruin. Only two doors remained, side by side. A visiting card—KATZ/MONCRIEFF FINE ART—was pinned to the blistered plaster wall.

Music played behind the door, a generic cocktail jazz. Fred knocked and waited, looking around and up to the stained low ceiling. The building would have a flat roof, probably tarred, leaking. This day's rain showed in the ceiling. Fred knocked again. No response. He jingled Geist's keys and decided, "No. Beyond curiosity, there's no reason to do it. It's too much risk. If they're in there, they assume I'm management, here to catch them cooking string beans, and throw them into the street.

"Malcolm X got it right. You hear the radio, you worry somebody's home."

Felice Beamer's door gave him no response either, though he called out her name and his after he knocked. She was away or she was busy. She'd asked him to call and come back, if only to pick up the money he'd earned, throwing her over and over again into the camera's field.

As Fred walked down to Jacob's floor a heavy rage surfaced in him that had been building all day, as if, nearing the artist's workplace, he were once again to have the power of life and death over Armand Kordero. By the time he let himself into Jacob Geist's dark studio, he was shaking with hatred against that sick purveyor of human lives, hopes, souls.

"He made you a slave, Jacob," Fred said to the old man in the darkness. "But you stole your soul back. I wanted to kill Armand Kordero for you. Or for myself. Or for humanity. Except I have promised myself no more killing. That ridiculous Shep! I tried to tear him in half! I had nothing against him. It was Kordero I hated. Enough killing. Enough killing. I could not face Molly again, or Terry, or Sam.

"In my heart I'm one of the villains. We make hell for each other. Buchenwald, Sobibor. The Limbourg brothers knew it, saw it, even suffered it. Philip the Bold had to buy those two boys out of jail."

Fred found that he was at the old man's hot plate, considering making a cup of tea for himself, as if by old habit, as if he belonged here. The city sky, augmented by the floods and spots from the Navy Yard, put enough light into the wall of windows for Fred to see his way around the studio, and even to make out the salient details of the Tibet map drawings that lay along the table. Months of labor. At the foot of one of them Geist had scrawled, *Honey will do it*. Other than the mattress and the hot plate, everything in here belonged to Armand Kordero—even the blank paper—

because of the deal Kordero had struck with the artist, without which Geist could do no work. He could not afford to.

"Philip the Bold," Fred said, "meet Armand Kordero. John, Duke of Berry, meet Armand Kordero. Jacob Geist, you sap, meet—what were their names? Herman and Paul and Chico Limbourg."

He'd wandered back to the hot plate while he mused, and put water on for tea. He could think here. Elsewhere got crowded. Here he could surround himself with the eccentric benevolence of Jacob Geist's imagination. Was that it? Eccentric benevolence? It was more impertinent risk, that of the free spirit. Complaining, Molly had called Fred that not long ago: free spirit—as if it were something between an insult and an enviable quality.

"Jacob, you poor son of a bitch; you owned not even the drawings you were going to make," Fred said. He poured water onto one of Geist's tea bags, in the mug he had washed last time he was here. "What's more, Kordero told you he refused to finance the Tibet project. You had to do it, being who you were. You couldn't finance it yourself, since you had nothing. You could not sell your own work, even if you could find a market for it.

"What did you do with the missing Bible, Paul and Herman and whatsis Limbourg? Did you steal your own work while Philip's sick body was attracting the first bold flies?

"Jacob? Where does that million dollars worth of parchment come from?"

The knock on the door was not timid. It was repeated until a female voice called, "I hear you talking in there, Jake. Open up, you bastard. Jake, I hear you."

Chapter 25

"Beamer, relax. It's me," Fred said, stepping quickly past her and pulling the door closed after him. She'd been struggling so hard to get in when the door opened that he was obliged to sweep her backwards several paces into the corridor. He locked the door while Beamer got her balance.

Fred said, "What's between you and Jacob Geist?"

"More like, how come you're in his place?" Beamer said.

Fred grinned and shook the handful of keys.

"Oh, shit!" Beamer said. "You're a goddamned spy. Next thing you do, you carry the information back to the owner in Chicago that I'm living here, right? And I'm out on my ass, right?"

There was almost no light in the hall. Felice Beamer was dressed in dark clothes, black pants and sweater, like a nun who had taken the vow of poverty seriously. She'd been carrying a bag of groceries that she'd put down by the door when she went to knock.

Fred said, "The futon, the hot plate, the toothbrush, the sausage—that's all between you and me, Beamer."

Felice Beamer pressed against the corridor's far wall. "Go on," she said. "If what?"

Fred shook his head. "The world being what it is, and people being the bastards they are—no, let's be honest: men being the bastards they are—you notice that I am in a position to offer a trade. Sorry about that." He shrugged. "At such a moment, civilization leads us to think first of forced sex, because I hold power over your livelihood and your place to live, and you have a powerful drive both to live and to work."

Felice Beamer turned suddenly and started down the hall, toward the stairway. "I'll have my stuff out by morning. Go ahead. Tear the fucking place down."

Fred sat on the floor and called, "Hey, Beamer, I don't want anything from you." She turned, hesitating. "You're not going to trust me, are you," Fred went on, "unless I let you give me a bribe."

"You sneaky bastard. Get this through your thick head. I'm not sleeping with you."

"Fair enough," Fred said. "I was going to suggest: when those photographs come out, choose one for me. I'd like to see how we did. Is that a fair bribe? Maybe you sell them for too much money and you'd rather not. But if you want, stick one on your door with my name on it. I'll pick it up some time."

"That'll cover it?" Beamer asked.

"Don't even do that if you don't want to," Fred said. "I'm curious, and I thought it might make you feel better. Don't worry about it."

"I'll give it some thought," Beamer said. She noticed her bag of groceries, on the far side of Fred.

"It's really the super, Jake Geist, I'm looking into," Fred said. "What I'm doing next, I'm going to that little dive on Bob Street and have coffee. If you want, meet me there and let the cruel world buy you a meal, and talk to me about Jake."

"Rita's is better," Beamer said. "I'll put my things away. It's all photographic supplies in that bag. Give me a half hour, forty-five minutes. If I'm not at Rita's in an hour, I'm not coming."

Beamer allowed the cruel world to buy her the largest meal she could think of, building around the central concept of an enormous steak. "They'll give me a doggie bag," she explained. "As long as management is buying. Waiter! Another Guinness!"

Fred had taken a booth near the kitchen area, where the noise of cooking and the exchange of shouted orders and recriminations would give their conversation cover. He drank his coffee and admired Beamer's style of attack against a dish of fried onion rings.

"What do you have against Jake?" Fred asked. "You mind letting me try one of those rings?"

"Be my guest. What I have against Geist? He's sneaky. He won't let you see what he's working on. He's a lousy super. They should let me do it. Also I loaned him a hundred dollars I can't spare, which according to him he was going to pay back Saturday. Threatening, you know, to claim I'm living there. Which is blackmail. The son of a bitch has been in and out, I know. But there's no sign of my money. He's dodging me."

She pushed the onion rings toward him to make space for the arriving platter from which rose the tantalizing steam of seared fat.

"What did Jake need the money for?" Fred asked.

Beamer had cut through the center of her steak and checked its color. Now she sliced a bite-sized corner from one of the pieces, shaking her head. "All I can tell you, he borrowed seventy dollars from me, saying he'd give me a hundred back on Saturday. Which he didn't, which is why I didn't have money to pay you last night, when I thought you were Bob, Richard's friend; which is why I just now had to borrow fifty dollars from Richard for gro…for developer and contact paper and all that.

"Me, Jake does not tell what he is doing." Beamer addressed herself to her plate.

Fred tried, "Who'd come to see him from time to time?"

Beamer chewed and shook her head. Fred ate another onion ring.

"You know Bob Ross on TV?" Beamer asked. "Paints the fuzzy little clouds and the happy trees and the rest of it? Like paint by numbers for people who can't count past three? Bob Ross? The frugal painter?"

"Can't say I do," Fred said.

"Any picture you want, he paints it in half an hour," Beamer sneered. "So long as he doesn't have to draw anything. That leaves empty landscapes, which is all he does. Say you want a cat with a bowl of goldfish? The man'd be in big trouble."

"Or the subjects you work with," Fred said. "The human figure. We got off on the wrong foot, and it's my fault, but I do enjoy your work, Beamer. I was—well—proud to be part of it, even though I was really doing something else."

"Snooping," Beamer agreed.

"On Jake Geist."

Beamer downed a couple of inches of Guinness and wiped her mouth with a yellow paper napkin. "The only people it looked like he ever might have talked to," Beamer said. "Those painters on the top floor? The ones I was telling you about?"

"You were?"

"Yeah. They paint like Bob Ross. You can't tell one from the other. What's more, they sell their shit. You see it in malls. *Krieff*, they sign it. The stuff is everywhere. You've seen it."

"Maybe I have," Fred admitted. "Krieff, hunh?"

"You've been in there, haven't you?" Beamer asked.

"Not yet."

"They're day people," Beamer said. "I'm a night person: work at night, think at night, live at night. This is practically my breakfast. I noticed Jacob Geist goes up there a lot, and it isn't to sweep the halls. It isn't to fix anybody's sink or those big vats we use to bathe in if we don't have a friend like Richard with a shower he lets us use.

"So he maybe confides his inmost secrets to the BobRoss twins. Maybe they tell him the story of their life, if any. I don't know. What do I know? Or he's into extortion up there. I don't know. All I know is he spends hours up there with them, and if he borrowed money from me, with menaces, which he did, who knows what he was up to with them. You think he would tell me what he was doing there? You think they will? Go ahead, talk to them. But they will clam up on you if they even open their door. They know you people are only looking for an excuse."

Fred said, "They're morning people, you say?"

"About six in the morning, when I'm ready to turn in, they start flushing and running water upstairs. They go out for their coffee. I don't know where they go. Diner somewhere. You're not eating. Don't you want to order dessert? I'm going to."

"In case I bump into them some morning, which is which? Between Katz and Moncrieff?"

"I've seen people eating the frozen strawberry shortcake, which is what I'm going to have," Beamer decided. "Katz is the woman. Isabel. She's older than you are, sixty maybe, kinda stocky, always wears a dress, never pants. She wears a smock when she paints, and a beret, if you can believe it. He's older. She calls him Buddy. Gray hair and a pointed beard. You'll know them because they're together. They're always together. If you're on the stairs about six-thirty in the morning? Seven? You'll catch them."

"I might take your advice," Fred said. "Order what you want for dessert and I'll pay the check. Take your time. Jake didn't drop a hint where he was going?"

"I almost peed when it was you coming out of his studio," Beamer said. "You scared me. He's already kind of a scary guy, being so secretive. Then when it was you in there, well, I thought—and he's foreign, too. Did I say that already? He's from Germany, talks with an accent—well, it scared me is all I was going to say. Like something walking over my grave, though my plan is cremation and throw it all out of a plane."

Chapter 26

Fred parked in Molly's driveway and entered the house through the garage, by way of the kitchen door. He moved quietly. It was late enough that the children should be sleeping or pretending to sleep. Ten-fifteen—Molly might be asleep herself, though the lights burned in her living room. He poked his head through the connecting door from the kitchen. She was there, in her mostly blue and white living room, wearing her blue bathrobe, lying on the couch, with a copy of the *National Geographic* flopped on the floor next to her. Her eyes were closed.

"Hey, honey," Fred said. Her face was wet with tears when he kissed her cheek. "Molly. Sweetie. Honey, what's the trouble?"

"I fell asleep," Molly said. She stretched, wiped her eyes, and smiled.

"Please tell me what's been bothering you," Fred said. "It's like a big thing that shouldn't be there sits between us."

Molly shook her head and sat up. "Sad dreams. Everything's fine." She wiped her eyes again and smiled again.

"You have a choice between tuna fish and Italian," Fred said. "Hot peppers, mayo, the works; on both of them."

"Not hungry. Thanks, though. That was sweet of you. It turned out the deal at Terry's school, which she hadn't told me, included a spaghetti supper I had to eat, though the kids and I had already eaten. Sit with me. I don't want to go to bed. Not yet. I've hardly seen you. I hardly know you any more. Tomorrow morning I'll choose one and take it to work for lunch, and cut the other in half for Sam and Terry. It'll save me starting the day by making all those lunches. God, is it only Monday?"

Fred sat next to her and put an arm around her shoulders. She winced away, but not entirely. "How'd it go at the open house?"

"Don't tell her I said so, but I have to admit, I agree with Terry," Molly said. "That Mrs. Holtzclaw is a prize double *j* double *e* double *r* double *c* double *k* jerk."

"The home room teacher?" Fred guessed or recalled.

"She's dressed up like the Avon lady and she wears free samples of everything she sells. She smells like a birthday party for six-year-old girls. She is, as my mother might put it, the Alpha and Romeo of applied bad taste. Except Mom wouldn't know bad taste if she sat in it. Come to think of it, neither did I, before I met Mrs. Holtzclaw.

"Terry sees right through her. She kept nudging me, stage whispering, 'See?'"

"It's going to be a long year for Terry," Fred said.

"Don't start giving her advice how to get along with jerks," Molly warned. "Let her learn to keep her head down and her opinions to herself until she gets home. How was New York?"

"That damned Kordero," Fred said. "His gallery's built on the company store model." He chuckled. "I can't help laughing. Our boy Jacob Geist diddled him. Needing seed money, he had sold the rights to everything he ever made to Armand Kordero, then he ran off with it all. He was in Charlestown, hiding out with the stolen goods, in a studio space he got free, while he made more works that, as soon as he made them, were also *de facto* stolen."

"That can't be legal," Molly objected. "Kordero's part of it, I mean. Can it?"

"I might not know legal if I sat in it, to use your term of art," Fred said. "I told you what Geist was working on when he died?"

"I might not have heard," Molly admitted. She inched the rest of the way out from under Fred's arm and turned to lie down again, resting her legs in his lap, her head on the arm of the sofa.

"I may be the world's expert on the work of Jacob Geist," Fred said. "As political theater, the stunts he pulled together, I guess, have merit. Are they art? I don't know or care. It's the drawings I care about. I spent hours with them. I feel as if I'm just starting to comprehend. They're how he thinks while he's planning the logistics of a campaign.

"As a for instance—the next project was to be a border drawn along the boundary that used to separate China from Tibet. Since that part of the world is all crags and impossible passes, and death to anything but yaks and an exceedingly sure-footed lichen, that border was never much better than imaginary anyway—but once upon a time, there was a country named Tibet. Now, because China is sitting in it, there is not.

"So, once again, Geist planned to inscribe an imaginary line onto the world. The first medium he chose to draw with was pollen—saffron, to be exact. This I learned from his notes written on the drawings of Tibet's geographical features. It's a privilege to oversee the man's mind working. Saffron, being gold in color, and also used to dye the robes of Tibet's priests…"

"And so fiendishly expensive," Molly interrupted, "that you could trade my weight in saffron for the John Hancock building."

"Cost did not strike Geist as an impediment," Fred said.

Molly said, "Saffron's the pollen of the autumn crocus. A pinch makes enough color and taste to fill a pot of rice, say, if you're making paella. They keep it behind the cash register, along with the caviar. Sounds like Jacob Geist was indulging in a poor man's dream."

"I want coffee," Fred said. He lifted Molly's legs to slide out from under them. "I need to be in Charlestown early tomorrow. Really early. Six-thirty." He started toward the kitchen.

"You saw my note about Hannah Bruckmann?" Molly asked. "On the kitchen table? She wants you to call her."

In the kitchen, while the water heated, Fred put the two wrapped sandwiches into the fridge and looked, without success, for anything he could eat without making what might seem to be a point.

It was too late in the evening to telephone Hannah Bruckmann. "I'm going upstairs a moment," he told Molly. "Get the kettle if it goes off before I'm down."

He knocked gently on Terry's door and poked his head in. She was a completely covered lump in a bed she kept piled with horse books and rocks. The rocks contained fossil microscopic organisms, according to Terry, exactly like the dubious proofs of life in the Mars meteors. Next to the bed the empty goldfish bowl yawned in reproach, awaiting the moment when Molly would relent and let Terry undertake the pet Molly must then look after. Given the room she kept, Terry, like Jacob Geist, was a subversive landscape artist. Not loudly enough to wake her, but loudly enough for her to hear if she was faking sleep, Fred told her good night.

Downstairs the kettle screeched. The house was too small for anything to happen in it that someone would not notice. Fred tapped at Sam's door and opened it after Sam's sleepy, "Yes?"

Molly kept at Sam but it didn't really work. Unless they were on him, no shoe he owned could stay within thirteen feet of any other. Clean clothes lay on the floor, mixed with dirty ones. Only the baseball cards Sam treasured and traded showed any kind of order, in that those he believed had value, or potential value, went into plastic view sheets which, in turn, flew here and there around the room.

"Did your teacher go for the snakes?" Fred asked.

Sam had the covers pulled up to conceal the fact that he had gone to bed in his clothes. He had the bedside lamp turned off to conceal the fact that until Fred knocked, he had been reading *Wars of the Tyrant Queen*.

"Mom made me do it over," Sam said. His voice was filled with ambivalent resentment. On the one hand, in a struggle between Fred and his mother, he was going to take his mother's side. On the other hand, on account of his mother, he'd been forced to write the composition twice.

"Too bad. I happened to see the first sentence. I thought the snakes were a good idea."

"I did too. But, well, it kinda went on from there. Mom said…"

Whatever Molly had said, Sam clamped down on it.

"Some teachers don't have a whole lot of imagination," Fred remarked. "You can get in trouble when they suspect you're making fun of them. I didn't think about that."

"I wish…" Sam said. Fred waited until it was clear that Sam was not going to develop the idea aloud.

"I do too," Fred said. "A lot of times I don't even realize I'm doing it."

"I have to sleep now," Sam said.

A moment after Fred had closed Sam's door the light glowed under it.

"What's doing in Charlestown so early tomorrow morning?" Molly asked.

"Probably nothing," Fred said. He took the cup Molly had filled for him. She'd carried his coffee and hers to the living room and put them on the table where Fred liked to rest his feet when he sat on the sofa.

"You called Hannah Bruckmann?"

"Tomorrow is soon enough," Fred said. "I have a right to spend a peaceful moment with you, don't I?"

"She said it was urgent," Molly rebuked him.

Fred put his feet up and sipped his coffee. "Other people's urgent is not necessarily my urgent," he said.

"She said call any time. Any time. As soon as you can. That's her home number."

"What I started to tell you about Jacob Geist," Fred insisted. "He decided after a while—once pollen was eliminated for whatever reason—he'd use honey. I love the sequence. Honey's still gold, right? In color. Still thematically connected to pollen, and flowers, right? The way he thinks, the practical invention—I love the man."

"Call Hannah Bruckmann," Molly said.

Chapter 27

"Oh, and also," Molly continued as Fred lurched upright again, "Clay called to say only that he intends to remain in New Haven for a week. That will be time enough, he says. For what he does not say. For you to accomplish whatever you need to accomplish, he says. He said to tell you he quite understands, and good luck. Call Hannah Bruckmann."

"Jeekers!" Fred said. He sat at Molly's feet, at the telephone end of the couch. "Hannah Bruckmann can't wait?"

"I quote," Molly quoted, "It's urgent. Tell Fred to call as soon as he gets in touch. I don't care what time of the day or night."

Hannah picked up on the third ring. "Does the name Mr. Geist mean anything to you?" she asked, once Fred had identified himself.

"I'll come now or first thing in the morning," Fred said. "Your choice."

"Wait. Does the name Asgar Jincks mean anything to you?"

"No."

"According to him he owns the parchment you showed me."

"I'll be right there," Fred said. "Where's *there*?"

"Brookline. I'm at the very dead end of Circle Street. Park in back. Come to the back door. I don't use the front."

"Half an hour," Fred said. He looked at Molly. "It's breaking open," he told her. "Or it's coming apart. Will you be all right?"

Molly demanded, "Why not? We were all right before you came."

Fred jumped as if she'd kicked him in the stomach.

"This evening, I mean. Tonight. Everyone minding her own business, the phone bill paid, the kids in bed without too many yells or tears."

"You sounded global for a moment," Fred said.

"You won't be back tonight," Molly concluded, "if you're hitting Brookline at midnight and Charlestown at six AM."

———

When Fred's car rounded Hannah Bruckmann's small house, lights flooded the drive and the leafy pocket of yard beyond the empty parking area. "She's gone, or she doesn't keep a car, or it's broken," Fred said. The building was a re-imagined carriage house, set aloof from an estate whose far edge was buried in woods. The prevailing scents in this part of the world were of privacy and money, but without ostentation.

Hannah was dressed for work, in the poncho and brown pants. She motioned Fred to come in from the lighted back porch, and to sit in the tiny kitchen off which a large un-lighted area gave a presentiment of careless living space.

The chair offered, one of a pair, was small and made of white painted metal, something deaccessioned from an ice cream parlor. It nudged a small round metal table from the same batch, on which Hannah had been writing notes, using a yellow pencil on a yellow legal pad. The pad was turned over so that only its cardboard back showed.

Fred said, "First, Mr. Geist. It's Jacob Geist. I do not know him. Also I did not know him. We encountered when Geist dropped that parchment. I picked it up, not realizing what it was. He died before I could return it. I'm crowded with guesses and inferences. The mind, which hates a vacuum, struggles to fill its vacancy with either logic or fiction, since it's still not strong on fact.

"As far as who owns it, all I can tell you for certain is, I don't."

"Also it never belonged to Sir Thomas Phillipps," Hannah added. "That narrows it down."

"As soon as you told me it had ludicrous value," Fred said, "and exceedingly clean people started beating a path to Clayton's door, I concluded that there was a time consideration. In truth it's not my problem. But I won't turn the problem over to anyone else, because I don't trust anyone else. From the little I've learned about him, I want to do the right thing by Jacob Geist. After I know the right thing to do with the parchment, I'll do it. Who's Asgar Jincks?"

"The Sam Walton of the rare book business," Hannah said. "He's blight and corruption with a big wide smile.

"This was and should be an old-world kind of business, where everyone can think about what's going on. His approach is equal parts FedEx and frenzy. Jincks is choking on money. His goal is to have a little office in every major city, where he likes to move in next to or underneath his closest competition. Rents an office the size of this kitchen, with two nice chairs, space to show six books, a modem and computer terminal and a youngster smart enough to tap into his central bank and not walk upside down by accident.

"Say you want what happens to be the only Andreas Aldobrandi *De Re Metallica* not in a public collection. We'll say you've been out golfing and it suddenly hits you you've got to have that book. You step into the Tucson, Arizona office of Jincks Fine Books, since you happen to be in Tucson, and you tell the pretty girl what you want. She taps it into her computer, Jincks' central bank finds it. It belongs to a widow in San Juan. The San Juan end goes after the widow at the same time as Jincks is quoting you a price. Next day, two days later—the transaction's completed.

"When Jincks sets his sights on your corner of the market-place, if he decides he likes you, he just crowds you out. If he hates you, and if you're a blamed fool, he buys a piece of you and you become the pretty girl with the modem. You've seen Jincks' ads in the *New York Times* and *Harvard Magazine* and everything in between."

Fred said, "This is a truly uncomfortable chair."

"I'm never here. Through his stooges, Jincks learned that I was doing research on the *Limbourg Bible*. After you and I talked Sunday—I couldn't reach you all day Monday, until you finally called—I received a telephone message from him at my office. Then this morning, by messenger, a certified letter from his lawyer says he'll take me to court if I do not immediately turn over the fragment of the *Limbourg Gospel*. Oh, yes, don't worry about a thing. He had it by name. Also he has photographs of the parchment you showed me, both sides, of which Xerox copies were included."

Fred said, "You want to show me the letter?"

"My attorney may or may not show it to you," Hannah said. "I won't."

"I'm going to sit on the floor," Fred said. "Otherwise I'll start to confess everything."

Hannah said, "My business is threatened. Do you under-stand?"

Fred sat on the kitchen floor, leaning against the wall next to the refrigerator, under a calendar three years out of date. "Geist already sold this thing to Walton? I mean, to Jincks?"

Hannah said, "It may make no difference. Jincks will browbeat and intimidate and cajole and bully and brag his way into it if it isn't his already. He's such a liar, I'd figured his talk about a Mr. Geist was a smokescreen. But it turns out Mr. Geist is a real person."

"*Was*," Fred said.

Hannah Bruckmann beat her fingers against the table top. "Does the rest of the manuscript exist?" she asked.

Fred shook his head. "It could be mixed in with a bunch of dirty socks and underwear. I don't know. The rest of what I don't know…"

"The Jincks approach," Hannah interrupted, "is to hit me on one side with the legal threat—which I don't care about except it wastes my time, since I don't have what he wants. But then he also called me at home three hours ago, on my unlisted number, and starts to explain what is about to happen to my business starting next week."

"I'll talk to Jincks," Fred said. "Where is he?"

"They always want to screw you over breakfast," Hannah said. "Copley Square Hotel. Coffee shop. Tomorrow morning. Nine o'clock."

"Maybe I'll happen to run into him," Fred said.

"You won't let Jincks have it?" Hannah said.

"Beyond I plan to meet the guy, I have no plan. What progress did you make on my research?"

"With Jincks in the picture, what difference does it make?"

"So you got something," Fred prompted.

"Nothing like research for pure good fun," Hannah said. "With Jincks pushing in, though, I don't know. I've got to protect myself. Maybe I'll give your check back, Fred, after breakfast tomorrow. Come by the office?"

"Better I make a third at breakfast. It's harder to screw two people at a time."

"You're joining us at the Copley?"

"Don't think I'm going to leave you alone with Asgar Jincks."

Chapter 28

"Old man without friends, carrying shabby luggage, they don't pull out all the stops to figure you out when you go under," Fred said, looking across at the quiet Lovett Shoe building. "Or else they're working like mad and they just have nobody on the force with Molly's genius."

When he surveyed the back of the building, Jacob Geist's floor showed no light. Felice Beamer's was blacked out. Only the two rooms on the third floor were lighted, where Isabel Katz and Buddy Moncrieff, the morning people, did their Bob Ross paintings.

Even at two in the morning, if they'd made the connection, the Boston or Charlestown cops ought to have a prowl car idling in the street. But for all the activity in and around the Lovett Shoe building, Jacob Geist might as well not have died.

Fred had first stopped at Chestnut Street and been told, by Bob Brewer on the desk, "Teddy's in your bed. Tell him to move over or move out. It's up to you," and Fred had recalled, "I have a place."

Once surrounded by the familiar gloom of the studio, Fred felt his way through the jumble of furniture until he found the old man's mattress. The eerie smell of the place was more intense around the artist's sleeping quarters. Fred rattled his keys, looked at the big double sink, and decided, "We'll see what an artist's crapper looks like. At the end of the hall, according to Beamer, at least hers is."

He left Geist's studio locked while he prowled to the end of the dim corridor, past padlocked doors. The end room's door was not locked. Once he discovered the hanging light pull, the room was discovered to be industrial in feel. Fifteen feet square, the room was dominated by a vat of galvanized steel, some ten feet long, five wide, and three deep. Three toilets stood together against the far wall of the room, perched like afterthoughts on a wooden platform pungent with rot. The shape of the room was so odd and so impractical, the vat must have pertained to operations carried out in a larger space now subdivided—tanning, or dying, or bleaching hides, or washing the workers' uniforms. "Or," Fred realized as he emptied his bladder into one of the chummy threesome of toilets, "that's how Beamer did those swimming figures I saw on her wall."

The vat offered only cold water. It would be a dismal bath, and a paralyzing swim unless the water sat for days during the hot months of summer. "Look at that, Fred. One evening's work and already you think like an artist's model."

Fred eased into the Asiatic fug of Geist's bedding, recalling the yak hair coat he had been grateful to borrow from a dead herdsman. Dead or, more exactly, tortured to death.

"Oh well," Fred said. He stared at the artificial light filling the windows over Jacob Geist's maps of Tibet's northern and eastern borders, asking himself, "How in the devil were you going to do it?"

He woke at five, having added the rank stink of his own night sweat to Geist's island of feral sleep. His voice as he woke, or that of Jacob Geist, was saying, "That's a lot of keys."

While he used the facilities at the end of the hall, he heard the pipes working elsewhere in the building. "Even a place this size won't keep a secret," he said. "Beamer's got that right." He made instant coffee on Geist's hot plate and carried it down to the loading dock, where he could sit and watch the building's entrance while the cold morning wind swept fog in from the Navy Yard, with gulls flying through it.

"What was the name of that bird that used to plague us in Tibet?" Fred tried to recall. "Black, with white markings, like a magpie, and a bloody eye. The best thief in the world."

By seven forty-five the couple of schlock painters still had not shown themselves. Fred checked their floor, heard their radio delivering itself of the morning news at that desultory sound level many couples like to keep permanent in their living quarters, as white noise. With Beamer's caution on his mind, Fred did not bother to knock. He did, though, stroll to the end of the corridor and take note that the couple was aggressively inhospitable. They'd installed a big padlock on their bathroom door, along with the sign KEEP OUT.

"We'll catch you later," Fred promised.

Jincks, his best lead yet, must even now be shaving and polishing his teeth, preparing himself to bruise and intimidate over coffee at the Copley Square hotel. Asgar Jincks, so far, was the first and only outside person who could put Jacob Geist together with the fragment from the *Limbourg Bible*. Jincks was the first and only person who had confirmed Hannah Bruckmann's speculation retroactively. The evidence was convincing. Jincks had dealt directly with Jacob Geist. He even had photographs.

———

They'd argued last night, before he left Brookline, how they should choreograph their part of the breakfast meeting. They'd finally agreed, over Fred's objections, this being Hannah's picnic and Fred the self-invited guest, that Fred would join the group only after Hannah and Asgar Jincks had their chance to say their first hellos.

Fred wandered into the Copley's breakfast resort at twenty after nine, locating Asgar Jincks by spotting Hannah Bruckmann. Jincks was a large middle-aged man with a vulgar pile of too much of his own gray hair. His skin was less gray than his suit. He looked like everyone's idea of a television program CEO. Pancakes, recognizing his importance in the world, had prostrated themselves before him, though he had not yet begun to torment them with his fork. He looked up, questioning, when Fred stood at the table.

"I represent Jacob Geist," Fred introduced himself.

"Oh, yes?" Jincks said. "Where has Geist been since Friday night?"

Fred pulled a chair from the nearest table and made himself comfortable. Hannah had only a cup of coffee in front of her.

"This is Fred," Hannah said. "I mentioned Fred would join us."

"If Fred has what I bought from Mr. Geist," Jincks said, "I don't understand how you're involved, Hannah."

Fred said, "Show me a bill of sale."

"Bill of sale? Are you joking? Where's Geist?"

Fred said, "He's out of this. But supposing I want to be fair with you, tell me the whole story: you, Geist, the Bible, the sale, the rest of it."

"What do you mean, 'Geist is out of this'?"

Hannah took a drink from her coffee.

"Put it this way," Fred explained. "I took over."

"And," Asgar Jincks confirmed, "you have the *Limbourg Bible*."

"Your story?" Fred repeated. He ordered coffee from a waiter who bowed between them.

Jincks said, "My story is I want what I bought."

"And then I say, prove what you bought, and prove you bought it," Fred replied. "While you're at it, prove who you bought it from."

With the side of his fork, Jincks put his pancakes out of their misery. He put a bite into his mouth. The room was well filled with people who could spend too much for breakfast.

"This is not the way I do business," Jincks said after he had finished his mouthful.

Fred said, "We know how you do business. The way *we* do business is, I ask you, when and where did you last see Jacob Geist?"

Asgar Jincks shook his head and took another bite.

"How much did you pay?" Fred asked. "For what, exactly?"

Jincks destroyed another contingent of volunteers from his plate. Hannah sat, intent, watching and listening. "You're fishing," Jincks concluded.

Fred said, "Show me a bill of sale and we will give it every consideration." He stood.

"What *we* are we talking about?" Jincks demanded. "You and this soon-to-be-retiring Bruckmann?"

Fred said, "I almost forgot. You bring up a side issue. Bruckmann says you threatened her." He waited for Asgar Jincks to make any motion that could be construed as response. "If she is disturbed," Fred said. "Or if her business is impeded, or if for example Jincks Fine Books ever sets up shop within three miles of her establishment, I will break one of your arms. Personally. Then, after a week has passed, I will break the other one. I tell you this not as a threat—I don't make threats—but as information you should have.

"Now. Another question. Those photographs. How do you come to have them? Finally, and for the last time, will you show me proof of purchase? You offered to take this lady to court. You must have something in writing."

Jincks clamped his lips together, pushing his plate away. "This much new input," he said, "I need time to process. How do I reach you?"

Fred said, "The way I do business is, I reach you."

Chapter 29

"I don't believe you have it," Jincks told Fred's back.

"You just wasted a lot of both of our time," Fred said over his shoulder.

"Then why did you come?" Jincks demanded with triumphant petulance.

Fred took two paces toward the table to remind him, "The side issue. The arm thing. You remember? One arm; then the other arm? Hannah, Jincks has nothing I want. False alarm. I'll call you."

⸺◦⸺

From a phone in the Copley's lobby Fred told Molly, "Join me across the street from your library, at Starbucks? Can you get loose from the reference?"

"I don't have time. Maybe you don't have time," Molly said. "I have some info for you. Jacob Geist was a very sick man. Truly sick. Dying. Cancer. He'd had one lung removed, and the other was going. Advanced cirrhosis of the liver. Occlusion of the arteries—he needed a quadruple bypass, but who would have attempted that, the state he was in? The man was a mess. He should have been dead long since."

Fred asked, "And he died of?"

"They think stroke."

"Gee," Fred said. "A natural death. They're sure? With all this commotion afterwards, in a world where people will kill for a hat, or a tattoo, or the price of a sandwich...."

"It's what Dee's contact reports," Molly said. She had to break off in order to answer a client's question about grasshoppers. Fred waved to Hannah Bruckmann as she crossed the lobby, too preoccupied to notice him.

When he had her again, Fred asked Molly, "Any word on what he was carrying? Luggage?"

"Nothing she mentioned."

"Or on the passport—other places he'd been?"

"Just France on the passport. But he could have gone on by ground to Belgium or other EEC countries, and not been stamped."

Asgar Jincks, emerging from the coffee shop, crossed the lobby and pressed the elevator's up button. He stroked the front of his suit jacket while he waited.

"He'd been gone four days," Molly said. "The same as you. Could be he was on the same plane over, on the seat next to yours."

"Anything else to notice? Large amounts of money? Address books? Papers?"

"I would have said. The reason I warn you might not have much time: based on *what* I don't know, they figured out he might be an artist."

"Really," Fred said.

"So in five more minutes they might get to Kordero's gallery," Molly said.

"And five minutes later, Kordero gives them me," Fred said. "Since I know where Geist's stuff is. He'll be out of his mind. Once he knows his artist finally is dead, Kordero wants to hit the world with a memorial exhibition as soon as the *New York Times* obit—which there is going to be. Geist is a good story. I'd better start moving." He hung up the phone and added, "Jeekers. Beamer reads the *New York Times*."

Hannah Bruckmann took his arm as he pushed from the Copley's lobby doors into the real world. "We'll sit in the park," she said. "I'll give you what I have so far." She kept hold of his arm until they'd forged across Saint James Avenue and into the park that keeps a proper distance between the Boston Public Library and Trinity Church. The carpet of grass was greener than usual on account of the fluttering presence of golden leaves everywhere. The sun had grown very bright.

"We'll sit in the sun," Hannah decided.

"You know this world," Fred said. "Was Asgar Jincks bluffing?"

"Of course. You were not?"

They walked in silence until they located a bench from which they had a view of water and trees and grass, and persons in delightful clothing, and people rushing to and from work, and architecture, and homeless people gathering cans and bottles.

Fred said, "I would love, for just twenty minutes, to forget the venal and troublesome jackasses banging their noses and asses against the glass jar I hoped I'd managed to drop around that beautiful thing. Heck, just five minutes I'd take willingly."

Hannah Bruckmann rummaged in her bag, saying, "I can only promise that the troublesome and venal jackasses who surrounded the Duke of Burgundy, Philip the Bold, are as dead as Philip is. That's where the story began. Once upon a time in 1402 Philip the Bold commissioned at least two of the Limbourg brothers to make him the story pictures for a magnificent bible. Then Philip died suddenly in 1404, before there was a chance the manuscript could be completed.

"One thing I found out, but it's what you call a side issue. A gang of scholars swears that manuscript I told you about, *Bibl. nat. fr. 166*, is the one Philip the Bold commissioned. Their reason boils down to the fact that this book was recorded as being in Philip's library later, along with some others I'd trade happily against a broken arm: the Coronation Master's *Clères Femmes* for example.

"Never mind. The point is, the book the Limbourg brothers were told to do was a bible, not just a *bible moralisée*, which is all *Bibl. nat. fr. 166* is. The scholars don't mind that the pictures in 166 are weedy and weak and nobody in the world's idea of a good time. You can't look at them and say Limbourg brothers with a straight face. They're dull, formulaic—never mind. Forget *Bibl. nat. fr. 166*, OK?"

"You got it," Fred said.

"In fact, forget everything," Hannah said. "Pretend we are starting fresh." She pulled out the Xerox copies of the photographs that Jincks' lawyer, looking to brag about his armaments, had sent. She pointed to the border around the text on the side of the *Hell* painting. "See these plants interweaving?" she asked.

"They sure are," Fred agreed.

"I mean, you see what the plants *are*?" Hannah said, striking the page with a trembling finger. "They are hops and nettles. Hops by themselves: well, maybe. Nettles by themselves, who cares? But both? It's incontrovertible proof, even without that initial."

Fred said, "I don't get it."

"Of course not. That's what I'm for. The hop was the special emblem of John the Fearless."

"John the Fearless," Fred began.

"Yes. John the Fearless of Burgundy, Philip the Bold's son and heir. The hop was his first emblem, and he added to that the stinging nettle. This was after his father had died, when John of Burgundy was pitted against his cousin, the Duke of Orléans, over the royal succession. It was a serious quarrel you really don't want to hear about, under a weak king, with armies drawn up and the two cousins striking scary postures across from each other, one saying, "I'll break your arm (Thank you for that, Fred), and the other responding…

"Anyhow, John the Fearless waving the nettle means, 'I'll sting you, cousin Louis.' To which Louis of Orléans replies by choosing a knobbed club with the motto 'I'll whack him,' for his people to wear, to which Fearless John responds with a badge for his people that represented a carpenter's plane, to shave down Louis's knobs.

"My only point is, the reason to celebrate all this self-congratulation, painting the hops and nettles around the page, is that the work is being done in the court of John the Fearless, and for him. Then…."

Hannah flipped the Xeroxed page back of another so as to point out the initial Clay had commented on.

"Inside that O there's John, baptizing in the Jordan river. You remember on Sunday I pointed out that tree done in gold leaf, and the animals holding up the letter? The lion and the eagle?"

"I recall that," Fred said. "At least in a general way."

"Well do. Because it's crucial," Hannah exclaimed. "We're lucky the sample page gave us evidence so clear and convincing. You remember that during all this time France and England are in the Hundred Years War?"

"Keep going," said Fred.

"So, forget that. I saw the white lion and I naturally thought Richard II of England, and I went tearing off in the wrong direction for an hour. But forget Richard II. Forget, even, the Hundred Years War."

"You got it," said Fred.

"The heraldic reference of that initial was to a Crusade—kind of a lame one. When John was just a kid, his father sent him off with an army to fight against the Muslim Turks, who'd gotten as far as Hungary. Therefore the famous story of the siege of Nicopolis, where John and his nobles, wearing wonderful clothes, were utterly destroyed by the Turkish Sultan,

Bajazet, the Thunderbolt. Those who weren't killed were cap-
tured and held for ransom, even John, whose ransom of two
hundred thousand florins was so high his dad had to borrow
it from an Italian money lender.

"A PR disaster like that, anyone in politics will tell you,
the only thing to do to live it down is either suddenly get
religion, which doesn't work for people who just lost a Crusade, or simply brag about it until it sounds good. So the
spin they put on it, everyone began to call young John, John
the Fearless. And Philip the Bold, proud father, deep in debt,
as if they had won the stupid war, founded a new Order of
Chivalry to *commemorate* the Nicopolis Crusade, especially
his loser son's heroic exploits. It was called the Order of the
Golden Tree and its emblem consisted of—follow this on
the page before you, Fred—a golden tree with an eagle and a
lion in white.

"It's why I say, forget Philip the Bold. Go straight to the
library of John the Fearless."

"And move forward," Fred said. "I can't say it wasn't my
idea. At least it's fun...."

Hannah interrupted, "I've already found certain reference
to twenty-four existing manuscripts known to have been in
the library of John the Fearless. Of those twenty-four manuscripts—that's a lot of books for those days—the biblical
works are all accounted for. There's a *Bible historiale* he bought
for his wife in 1415, that's now in Brussels; also in Brussels a
New Testament of 1400 that had once belonged to Marie de
Berry. Also in Brussels there's an old *Bible historiale* from
1355, volume II only, that shows up in the 1420 inventory
of the worldly goods of John the Fearless, but as far as our
bible goes..."

Fred said, "Tell me when you get to the end of my five
thousand bucks. By then I should know if circumstances
warrant your continuing."

Chapter 30

While the last seven minutes on his meter digitalized away into the vacancy they had come from, Fred sat in his car and told himself, "There's no reason to stop by Mountjoy Street unless I want to add to my collection of business cards from curators and museum directors and heads of boards of trustees and collectors and lawyers and scholars. I'll turn them all over to Sam. In twenty years, what will a Philippe de Montebello card be worth in mint condition? A Malcolm Rogers? A Sam Fogg?

"Question: will Kordero see any gain to himself if he gives my Chestnut Street address to the law? Answer: he'll keep it informal, and send another goon. Question...."

A young woman, shivering in a thin dress the color of the majority of this autumn's falling leaves, her skin as dark as branches rained on, put a lovely round face into his driver's window. "Sorry. Are you pulling out?" she asked.

Fred saw, in his rear-view mirror, one of those mini U-Haul vans, poised in the road behind him in a spot from which she could command his space once he woke up and moved.

Fred said, "It's yours if you'll make a choice for me, between alternative A and alternative B."

"Go with A," the young woman said firmly. "At least half the time I find that works for me."

"You own a parking place," Fred told her.

"Next question," she added. "You have four quarters for a dollar?"

Fred fumbled in his pocket and pulled out his last quarter. "If you've got dimes or nickels, fine. Otherwise this is an advance against the next time I need your advice."

"Next time choose B," she said, accepting the quarter. "Your odds are about even that way too, but see, your instinct will be expecting A, since that's what you did before. With B, next time, you maybe get an edge."

"It's not like I'm *wanted* for anything," Fred reminded himself as he drove through the city toward Charlestown. "I've been sneaking around so long, I start to recall what it's like to be hunted. But I'm not being hunted, at least not by the law. I haven't done anything except to refrain from making some people's job easier. I'm hiding something that's worth more than the Lovett Shoe building. That may be a crime.

"How much trouble do I want to step into? When the uniforms finally start streaming into the Lovett Shoe building, and find me in the act of following that young lady's advice, what do I tell them? I'd have asked her that too, but I'd run out of quarters."

Fred cruised past the house on Chestnut Street and saw no sign of interest. Several long blocks away, Lovett Shoe also continued to exist in an island of calm. "It's unreal," Fred said, pulling his car into the curb at some distance from Geist's building. "As unreal and unlikely as mine being the hand old Jacob's last throw of the dice tossed the manuscript page into."

He clomped his car door closed and sauntered down the street, jingling Geist's fistful of keys. "The best I can do," he said, "is *Jake Geist was called away. He asked me to keep an eye on the building until he got back. Me being almost a neighbor, I said, why not? He should have been back last Friday. It looks like he got delayed.*

"That line should hold up for at least half an hour."

Climbing the stairs, he mused, "I reckon keys on this ring would get me into the first two floors, the freight elevator, the works. There's enough keys here to sink a cat."

Moncrieff and Katz had switched to a program that sounded like a game show. Fred knocked on the door that bore the neat KATZ/MONCRIEFF FINE ART card. He made a racket of firm authority, at the same time looking over the pair of locks, and selecting, from the ring, the couple of keys that seemed most likely.

"Mr. Moncrieff! Ms. Katz," Fred called. "Open your door, please. I'm from the super, Jake Geist." He listened, and talked more to them, until they had to know that one way or another he was coming in. He tried keys until he had the pair of locks, reassuring the whole time; then he opened the studio door.

Here was true industry, but with no sign of the artists responsible for it: no inhabitant scuttling for cover, or outraged interference, or terrified scrambling for the telephone. Fred trotted quickly through the two adjoining rooms, taking in, first, only the absence of human occupancy.

"Malcolm X was right," Fred said. "That radio buzz sounds like habitation. Think of it, our radio noise is going to persist for aeons after this planet has become a yawing cinder dragging a tail of poison ice. '*You're absolutely correct. The answer is Anne Estelle Rice,*' nobody will hear, for all that the words are floating ever outward in their own configuration of photons."

He left the hallway door open while he started looking through the place, "as long as I'm here. Haven't there been complaints of leaking?"

Each of the two rooms was laid out in an arid, businesslike way. Each had a wall, like Geist's, that was made of windows. This being the top floor, the ceilings were relatively low, only nine feet. In the room Fred had entered from the hallway, the one used as work space, two easels sat side by side—heavy wooden things designed in such a way that the paintings being worked on could be raised or lowered with a crank. Each artist had a rolling table covered with tubes of acrylic paint, laid out in neat rows next to a palette that had been scraped clean of the last mixed colors; the last squirts of pigments whose residual stains showed in the same order on each palette.

Each easel held a painting on stretched canvas two and a half by three feet large. There was a lot of knife work in both pieces. Painting A presented a lake scene, with a cabin in the middle ground, on a promontory jutting in from the right side, and clouds at sunset throwing color into the lake. It was signed Krieff. It was dry to the touch, but acrylic paint dries fast.

Painting B was a lifting wave seen from a sandy shore. The belly of the wave was blue-green, as if transparent. Its foaming crest reflected the active presence on the horizon of clouds at sunset throwing color even onto the wet sand. A sea gull, not officiously specific in its delineation, cruised in the crimson sky and was reflected, even less specifically, into the wave. This painting also was signed Krieff. It was dry to the touch.

The room smelled of plastic and the dryers that make acrylic paint last forever. Fred's stomach turned in nausea. The room contained five hundred paintings exactly like these two, in three sizes, and showing about sixteen variations. They were criminally cynical things done by talented people who knew better: ugly, like jewelry made for poor people. If your rented trailer home was in a shitty place, one of these, which you'd pay a week's wages for, was to give you the illusion of places you would rather be.

The paintings were stacked in racks made by a carpenter. Other racks held gilded plastic frames in the three sizes demanded by the paintings.

"Truly, truly gruesome," Fred complained, and forged into the Katz/Moncrieff living area. This was the room in which the radio hinted at humanity. The same size as the work room, this place had been furnished with no pretense that it was anything other than a room where people slept, cooked, ate, talked on the telephone, read magazines. It looked like the dormitory for reform school counselors. Other than a mirror over the deep industrial sink, nothing hung on the walls, whose plaster was painted gray. Two cots stood end to end along the wall farthest from the window. Under the window, positioned so as to command the view of Charlestown harbor— truly, from these windows, there was more than a lifetime of reality to paint from—two heavy leatherette recliners sat side by side.

The room held a rack filled with hanging clothes, a small refrigerator, electric stove, and a cupboard in which sat a supply of dishes. The sink was clean and empty.

"It's like the place was cleaned with a flame thrower full of Lysol. There's nothing human left. Nothing organic even. They live like they paint," Fred said. "Like a couple of robots. Couple? I can't even see that they're a couple.

"According to Beamer, Jacob Geist spent hours up here with these two people? What did they have? Food? Jokes? What could they offer powerful enough to overcome the instinctive loathing he'd have for the travesty of painting these two were knocking out? It's wrong. It's all wrong. Or else. Or else—what did they have he wanted?"

With a tension of creeping dismay, Fred began to poke around the room more closely. Nothing personal or intimate showed anywhere, not even in the top drawer of either bureau. It was as if each member of the couple who had conspired to achieve the Krieff identity, had lost track of who he was in life. Both beds were made. No loose sock or soiled pair of underpants suggested the raunchy aspects of identity. It was not even possible to judge which bed was occupied by the man, and which by the woman. They slept head to toe, as if they were on a train going to the generic destination of one of their paintings: *Sunset Lake* or *Evening's Afterglow*, or *Little Home in the Valley*.

"Gad," Fred concluded. "Who are these people?"

Isabel Katz, Buddy Moncrieff, please call me, he wrote on a piece of paper. He added the Chestnut Street number, and the name Fred. Then he thought about it for twenty seconds before he crumpled the paper and stuck it in his pocket.

"Maybe not," Fred decided.

Chapter 31

As long as he had this opportunity, he shouldn't waste it. Fred trundled down the stairs to the third floor and scouted the corridor, surveying the padlocked doors next to and across from Geist's studio. Though it would have been quicker using his native skills, it would not do to be caught jimmying padlocks. So Fred took the time to locate the appropriate key to the lock on the door opposite Jacob's studio.

"You rascal!" he exclaimed in pleasure when he pushed the door open into the storeroom. "Son of a bitch! You've already gotten started! Sick as you are! Good for you, Jacob!"

The room was filled, almost to the ceiling, with compact stacks of white five-gallon plastic buckets bearing black generic labels identifying their contents: HONEY. In a windowless room almost twelve feet square, it must be tons of honey.

"It's amazing," Fred told Molly on the telephone, calling from the Store 24. "The drive of the man, the arrogant discipline. Here he is on the lip of the grave, and he knows it, and he goes right on with his work—sticks with the cigarettes and vodka, knowing he's a condemned man, and starts collecting honey. I'm so in love with the guy I'm flummoxed. How much would a bucket of honey cost—the big size like Dunkin' Donuts would order?"

"It's lunch time," Molly said. "At least—well, it's late, but I haven't eaten. Can you join me?"

"I was thinking," Fred said, "I'd love you to see the man's drawings, and his studio. Do you have time? Can I pick you up?"

"He sounds like a free spirit," Molly said. Her voice was wary and distracted. Wasn't that a recurring theme in her vocabulary of accusation these days? Free spirit? Usually accompanied by a pang of—was it jealousy? Because Fred was not tied as she was? Devoted, yes; and loyal: but not tied.

"As free as your spirit can be when you're dying of cancer," Fred said. "Also poor, and hunted, and can't own your own life work. Maybe you'd call him a free spirit."

"Don't be angry," Molly begged. "You were saying, about honey?"

"I'll swing by the library," Fred said.

"Maybe we'd better stick to the telephone for now," Molly said. "You've gotten so irritable…"

Fred dropped more change into the phone's box while he gazed at all the rejoinders he would not use, none of which would provoke either gentleness or reason. Then, "Honey," he started.

"Yes. Honey. You began telling me about Jacob Geist and honey. It's your subject. You raised it."

"I was interrupted," Fred started.

"That is the nature of conversation," Molly scolded. "Conversation is not a series of lectures."

"Jeekers," Fred said. "The sentence I began intended to continue, I was interrupted by the photographer from the next floor up, so I couldn't examine more than three of the rooms. Each contained tons of honey. Geist had made a good start toward collecting enough to draw that boundary."

"And what did he say?" Molly asked.

"Who?"

"The photographer. When he interrupted you," Molly said.

"The photographer said, So that's what Jake has been doing with the freight elevator he won't let anyone else use," Fred told her.

"Fred?"

"Yes?"

"Sorry to lose my temper at you."

"I'll be there in fifteen minutes."

"I don't know if there's time now," Molly said, tears in her voice.

"Molly, is it trouble at work?"

Every now and again some small-minded blowhard city counselor forgot the town's business was to promote good services for its citizens, and began campaigning for intrusive civic selfishness by threatening the livelihood of any Cambridge employee who couldn't afford to live in the city on account of its punishing rents and real estate costs.

"Fred, never mind..." Molly began.

"I'm out of change," Fred said, and clicked off.

The library's parking lot was crowded. Fred was obliged to forage along Broadway for several blocks until he found an open meter. Molly, he was told by the folks at the desk, had gone for lunch.

"It's three o'clock," Fred said. "Did she mention where she was going?"

The folks at the desk agreed that she hadn't.

Fred blundered out to the library's front steps and cast his eyes around. Molly normally brought lunch with her. In fact, hadn't she planned to bring Fred's sandwich today?

It was chilly, but not too chilly to sit outside if you wore enough clothes. The park lying between the library, the high school, and Broadway was not large enough for anyone to hide in. Fred plodded quickly through it, in case Molly had found a corner to be alone in—though normally she was a gregarious soul, and would have company at lunch. There was no sign of her among the group of high school kids, the mothers and nannies pushing children in strollers, the homeless who made this corner of Cambridge their home. So she'd gone to stretch her legs and let off steam, or she had an errand to do—or whatever.

Fred bought a slice of pizza from the truck parked at the high school, and he sat in the sun, on a bench, eating it while he watched for Molly's return.

"Whatever it is that's bugging her, I could at least keep her company," Fred said. "It's what she seemed to have in mind."

Twenty minutes after the pizza was finished, Molly walked toward him along Broadway, from the direction of Harvard Square's cluster of commerce and academy. She was wearing an old pea jacket over a navy skirt. Her head was uncovered, her scuffed brown leather bag swinging. Fred had tried many times to replace it, but she refused. "It fits me," she said when he raised the subject. She walked briskly and efficiently, so preoccupied by whatever was on her mind that she would not have noticed Fred if he hadn't called, "Molly?"

She turned back, startled, and blushed like a child caught stealing.

"Join me a minute," Fred said. "I saved us a good bench."

Molly stood hesitating, clutching the coat and the bag against her. Then she sat next to him, on the edge of the bench. "I was thinking maybe we would spend the evening together," she said. "Mom says she'll feed the kids and sit with them until I get back, if it's not too late."

"Where shall we go?"

"Some place quiet," Molly said.

"There's always Salt Lake City," Fred suggested.

"Too far," Molly said. "It sounds good, though."

"I'll take you to Charlestown," Fred decided. "I want you, if the boys in blue aren't all over it by now, to see Jacob Geist's studio. For one reason, just because I want you to see it. But also, sitting here, I was thinking I'm about to give up. Unless you can see or suggest something else I should do, I might as well tell Boston PD what Geist's last address was. I hate to do it. I hate putting in motion a sequence that leads to Armand Kordero getting his clammy hands on Geist's drawings, and so easily. I hate…who cares what I hate? I'd really appreciate, Molly, if you could apply your instincts to the place before I give up."

"It's not like you to give up," Molly said.

"I'm a volunteer. My concern is only to see that the parchment, since I had an accidental fiduciary responsibility for it, doesn't get into the wrong hands. Either I keep control of it, or I have it locked in a safe deposit box with the Attorney General holding the key, or—I don't know. I have my life to lead, my own business to take care of. If I put much more time into this, it's because I'm blinded by ego and self-indulgence.

"But also—this happens to scholars too sometimes, even the most venal among them—I have a great admiration for Jacob Geist and for his work, his big defiant plan to set the People's Republic of China on its ear."

"Affection can lead to mistakes in judgment," Molly agreed.

"I wish I'd known him, been in his confidence," Fred said. "I'd have loved to ask him—sitting here watching those golden leaves trickling like water out of the trees, and waiting for you, I was wondering how the devil an artist thinks. He has to mix outrageous intellectual cockiness with practical know-how. He's got to think like Montgomery and operate like Patton. Forget how he's going to lay his border down across mountains and glaciers and valleys all of which are killers, in the face of the Chinese army, all of whom are killers—how can Geist fly that much bulk anywhere surreptitiously?

"Molly, here's a question…"

Molly said, "Then you're free this evening?"

"We'll have dinner at Rita's. We'd better both have our cars, in case something comes up. You have an hour before you're off, so I have time to case Mountjoy Street for mail. My question, trying to get into Geist's head: honey must be eighty percent water, wouldn't you say?"

Molly heaved a deep sigh. "I can find out."

"It doesn't matter, the percentage. The theory—the liquid from sugar cane, boiled down, makes powder, which is like pollen. Can you distill the liquid from honey and get powder? That would be so much lighter, was my thought; so much easier to transport in quantity...."

"I'm due at the desk," Molly said.

"Tell you what. Six is early to eat," Fred said. "We'll meet on Arnold Street. Pull in behind my car where you see me parked. In case anything's going on."

Chapter 32

Parked far enough up Arnold Street to keep track of the preternatural calm that continued to prevail at the Lovett Shoe building, Fred had been keeping his eyes equally on the rearview mirror. When Molly's red Colt pulled in behind him, he climbed out in time to get her door open.

"Your place on Chestnut Street's not far, is it?" Molly asked.

"Five minutes," Fred said.

"We'll go there first," Molly declared. "It's where you've got that parchment, isn't it? The one I'm expected to take care of when you disappear into the wasteland?"

Fred said, "Had I told you?"

"Let's have a look," Molly demanded. She had stayed behind the wheel and she motioned Fred to get in next to her. Fred did so, saying, "And after, we'll eat at Rita's."

Molly eased into the traffic and, following Fred's directions, threaded under the stanchions and shadows of the bridge supports, poked up and down the steep one-way streets, and maneuvered the distance to Chestnut Street, where she parked expectantly.

"Not that I don't trust my colleagues here," Fred said, remaining in his seat: "but ignorance is sometimes the best camouflage."

"Don't I know it," Molly said.

"I don't want to lay that thing out for all and sundry."

"Meaning?" Molly asked dangerously.

"It's not smart to open it out in the car. It's too large. We'll use the pool table if no one's in there, or my room."

"Your room," Molly reflected.

Fred opened his door. "Molly, you know I keep a bed here. I'm one of the owners of this building."

Molly followed him, moving around her car and across the street. Teddy, back of the desk, stood up when Molly entered the vestibule, and told her, "Hello, Molly."

The clicking of pool balls, and an exchange of laughter, issued from the back room next to the kitchen. Fred said, "We're going to violate a rule and go upstairs for a few minutes."

Teddy said, "OK."

Fred went around the desk to pull the *New York Times* package from the drawer. Molly stood staring at the Peterson painting of zinnias. "Where do I know that picture from?" she asked.

"We saw a transparency of it last winter," Fred said. "During the big snow. I forget now what month it was. On Newbury Street together, you recall? At Dmitri Signet's gallery?" Molly shook her head, looking. "The guy had a folder full of slides and photographs," Fred reminded her. "That's the one we said we wanted."

"And you found it," Molly said. She followed Fred up the stairs to the second floor, along the hall past the six bedrooms and the bathroom.

"Mine's in the front," Fred told her. "Over the stairs. Where they used to keep the baby in these houses, I guess, since it's called a borning room. I used to like looking down onto Chestnut Street some evenings. Teddy's sleeping here now. I'm not going to keep people from using it while I.... Molly, you'll notice my former living arrangements are on the plain side." He opened the door into a low room eight feet square, containing two windows, a radiator, a straight chair, a single mattress with a blanket, and four hooks on the inside of the door, holding towels, a plaid sport jacket, and Teddy's straw hat.

Molly looked around while Fred opened a window and straightened the blankets on the mattress. She smiled. "Now I understand," she said. "In your former life you used to be a nun."

"We'll open it on the bed," Fred said. "The people who know and love such things would hate me for what I'm doing, but I felt the circumstances were unusual." He slipped last Friday's paper from its blue plastic bag and laid it on the gray blanket.

"I like it here," Molly said. "I'd have a little table, maybe. Otherwise I wouldn't change a thing. But no, you're right. Add a table and the next thing you're wanting a cushion for the chair; curtains; bed pillows; sheets—no, this is better. Simpler."

Fred said, "I can't tell if you're joking."

"Show me the parchment," Molly said.

Fred opened the newspaper whose principal fold, along the spine, had recreated the folio's old crease. He'd protected the parchment in an envelope of opaque glassine paper from the supply in Clayton's storeroom area, and so it was not until he had set that aside that the spectacular color and clarity of the *Lazarus* stood out.

Molly knelt next to it and said, "Golly."

On Arnold Street again, as they walked toward the loading dock back of the Lovett Shoe building, Fred said, "What we're about to do is not legal. I've gotten used to it but that doesn't mean it's not breaking and entering."

Molly said, "It's your party, Fred." She brushed imaginary crumbs from the flank of her pea jacket with the hand that was not engaged with keeping her bag from swinging.

"No, here's the thing," Fred said. "Since your mom and Sam and Terry are expecting you later, you should have no inkling what the larger context is, if we're interrupted. I have keys. You are my guest. Beyond that, you don't need to know anything. In case someone official appears, I'll have to start to make things up, and chances are I'll at least find myself answering questions all night at the nearest precinct. So all you know is, I asked you to come look at Jacob Geist's studio. Are you willing?"

"Probably. But when you start making things up, I may need to start making things up also."

Unlocking the door next to the loading dock, Fred explained, "I haven't taken the time to go through all these keys. There have to be elevator keys, and god knows what kind of available space on the first two floors and all—but I'm used to the stairs."

Molly kept pace with him in the wide staircase. "Not that I've ever seen a shoe factory," Fred said. "And they've been scrapped or sold long ago, but the machines in that place must have been something else! Cutters and stitchers and lathes—what I don't know about machines would fill more than two floors."

"You don't have to entertain me," Molly said. "I am interested. I'm just quiet this evening."

In silence they climbed the rest of the way to the third floor, and walked the corridor. "If you need a bathroom," Fred said. "Before we go in—the studios don't have them. There's one down the hall."

Molly shook her head.

"So, shall we get on with this crime?" Fred asked. "Last chance to remain on the side of the angels."

Molly stood ready, clutching her bag. "Fred, it's decided," she said.

"We don't turn on the lights," Fred explained, opening the door and stepping back for her. They waited a moment to let their eyes adjust to the change of light. Fred went to the flashlight that was still lying in the artist's bedclothes.

"I prefer it this way," Molly said. "If you don't mind. Turn it off, OK?"

"The most recent work's along under the windows, the map drawings of Tibet," Fred said, moving toward them.

Molly stayed at Geist's doorway. "What I've been trying to tell you," she said. "I'm late...."

Chapter 33

"I missed my period a week ago."

"Hey," Fred exclaimed, moving toward her.

"Stay where you are," Molly said. "I can't bear it."

"There's a rocking chair if you want to sit," Fred said.

"I don't want to. I just don't want to be alone any more. Also I don't want to talk about it, do you mind? Because I can't bear it."

"Gee," Fred said. He trembled, next to Jacob Geist's sink and hot plate, the way a person who has been trudging through freezing mist does when he notices that one more step will take him over the edge. "Molly, you were so careful. Both of us were."

"If you'd said anything else," Molly began. "If you'd started with, *I* was so careful, Fred, it would be like losing an arm or a leg to do it, but I was going to walk away from you."

"But this means a hundred things to think about," Fred said. "When we know for sure. What will Terry think, and Sam? And, well, your mom, and are you…"

"I do not want to think about it or talk about it," Molly said. "I bought the EPT test this afternoon. My plan was to take it tonight if I could get away from everyone. Not knowing is an unbearable, burning itch, like the start of a urinary infection. It's been driving me crazy."

Fred said, "You still want this dark room between us?"

"I saw your small, bald room on Chestnut Street," Molly said; "with its small, bald, empty bed: and I was filled with envy." She walked warily to the rocking chair and sat in it, creaking slowly back and forth.

The icy chasm in front of Fred became very deep and very wide. Those scavenging birds he could not remember a name for screamed in it, half way down. "This probably isn't the place," Fred said. "I don't know what's involved. Shall we go some place and do it? The EPT? Shall we rent a room? What do you need? What do you have to do?"

"I pee," Molly said, shivering. "I can pee anywhere. It's not that." She rocked more slowly.

Fred moved cautiously toward her. "You know..." he started.

"I do know," Molly cut him off. "I wish I was brave enough to do it this evening. I wish I'd been brave enough to do it on my own."

"This might be braver," Fred said.

"Not knowing is bad," Molly went on. "Knowing could be so much worse. My life upside down."

"You've been—kind of remote," Fred said.

"Yes, you have," Molly said. She rocked until Fred came to her, knelt next to the chair, and put a hand on hers where it rested on the chair's arm. The weight of its presence upset the rhythm of the chair's movement.

"If it's what you want, and if I could, I'd give you that room," he said. "I don't know how I could stand it. For as long as you need. And, if you trust me to, I'll watch out for the kids. I've got some money saved, so I don't have to work, and..."

"Fred, let's look at these drawings, since we're here," Molly said. "I won't do the test tonight. It's better tomorrow morning, maybe the next day. Tonight we stop thinking about it."

"I don't stupidly ask, are you sure you counted correctly?" Fred asked.

"A million times. What do you think I do when the kids are in bed?"

The stillness in the room was interrupted only by the creak of Molly's unbalanced chair. Fred's hand on Molly's was silent. Molly's open-eyed tears were silent, reflecting the golden haze of light from the windows above Geist's maps of Tibet. Finally Fred said, "I'm going to say the wrong thing."

"Yes?" Molly said.

"You give me more pleasure than I knew there was."

———

Molly insisted that she be the one to hold the flashlight as they walked along the drafting tables Geist had constructed.

"I've gotten to know these drawings better," Fred said. "It takes a while. They're intricate. They feel complete. But I can't tell if Geist feels—felt—they are finished. They're not signed, but most of his things aren't signed. The way he works, it's as if he was keeping all this series in the air at once, working a little sepia color in one day, scratching out lines another day. He's indulging himself to the extent that though they're a series, each is a unique work of art that should fly on its own."

"The talk about skulls is alarming," Molly said, pointing to the notation concerning filling the skull cup with pollen.

"It's standard in Tibetan iconography," Fred said. "Sometimes priests drink from cups made out of human skulls. Those, or fake ones, used to be a big tourist item."

He pointed to the place where the artist had hit upon the idea of using honey.

"There's another set that has to do with the Line of Demarcation," Molly reminded him. "Can you find those in this archive? The boundary that separated Vichy France from the part of France occupied by Nazi Germany?"

"Those drawings were part of the group Jacob stole back from Armand Kordero," Fred told her. He led the way to the heavy storage shelves that the artist had erected along his studio's inside wall, using doors brought down from the vacated spaces on the fifth floor. He lifted a few drawings from the stack and laid them out on the floor where Molly could shine her flashlight on them.

"He thought of that line as the edge of a butterfly's wing," Fred explained.

"The significance of November 11, 1994," Molly said, "which you asked me to look up for you..."

"I did?" Fred asked. "Oh, yes. That was the date for which this work, the *Line of Fat*, was scheduled."

"That was the fiftieth anniversary of the date when the Germans decided, arbitrarily and unilaterally, to eliminate all pretense, and to erase their Line of Demarcation. For everyone living there, it was like lifting the barrier of sand that separates salt from fresh water.

"Fred, your man loved trouble. While you were here, I suppose you looked everywhere for things to explain where Geist had been, and how he came to be carrying that parchment?"

"I turned the place inside out," Fred said. "I looked at everything."

"Under the mattress? Underneath and between the drawings?"

Fred kept nodding his head.

"These matted drawings, the ones with acetate around them," Molly continued. "You opened all these up and looked inside?"

Fred shook his head.

"Well someone opened some of them."

It was fifty minutes before Molly, surrounded by her pile of clear plastic, said, "Here's something."

The drawing she held was of the area around Moulins, a city almost due south of Paris, through which the Line of Demarcation had passed when it was cut across the country in 1940. Up to now, they'd found nothing. Molly had stripped off the acetate, raised back the face plate of the hinged mat, and reached under this drawing as she had under thirty others. She pulled out a yellowed, transparent piece of paper covered with crabbed black writing that ran in perpendicular lines, the back crossing the front.

They'd both been working in the beam of the single flashlight, stacking the drawings on the floor. Fred put down the one he was unwrapping so that Molly could concentrate the light on what she had found. She told Fred, "I can't read it. I can't even tell what language it is."

Fred took it from her and studied it, both sides. It presented some of the unnerving and irritating feel of the Gothic lettering on the parchment, whose words refused to stand apart one from another.

"I've had so much practice at Christmas," Molly said, "seeing what the children had found and sneaked open: and so much practice a while ago sneaking packages open and trying to seal them closed again so Mom wouldn't know, since I hated surprises, like Sam. I was certain some of these had been messed with—and now we see…"

"I'm not sure I can read it without real light," Fred said. "Maybe not even then. Shall we take it with us to Arlington?"

Molly flipped the matted drawing onto its face and laid the paper she had found onto its creamy back, shining the flashlight on it. "We'll do it here," she said. "It's important, since Jacob Geist had hidden it. It's a letter. You're good at languages, Fred. Put this way, the other side stops interfering so much. Sit on this side, next to me. Pretend it's French, as I think it is—see? The heading now, I can read. *Ma chère Isabelle.*

They worked on it together, arguing over certain words that ran together, certain letters that could be several others, until they had a rough translation of the undated letter, which Fred read aloud.

My dear Isabel,

Never mind how, I learned of your existence, and that you are a young woman. I pass to you, since I am old and must be dying, the only inheritance I have to offer you. Keep this from your mother.

During the war I received an object from a refugee, a Jew of Poland, who hid with us before he was taken. He carried with him a painted skin from the old days, part of a book, he said, made by the brothers Limbourg. The book itself, he claimed, he had left with relatives in Warsaw, for safekeeping.

His name is not important. He swore on his parents' life that this skin was of great value. A treasure. But Jews lie. However, I have asked other people and it may be true. It is a painting, and shows Lazarus, a Jew.

The war ended. There were reprisals. I was watched. Your grandfather was killed. In truth, I almost lost my reason.

I shall be dead. If you or your representative will present yourself at my hotel, the Hotel du Lac, here, in the city of Moulins, presenting the token I enclose with this letter, the parchment shall be yours, and the fortune—if there is indeed a fortune. I do not believe it. But I am old, and dying; and still watched.

Do not speak to your mother of this. Do not speak to your mother of me.

I do not send my love. I do not know you.

> *Your Grandmother.*

Chapter 34

"Next, we find Isabel," Fred said.

"Why hide the letter?" Molly asked. "Why wouldn't Isabel take the letter itself, along with the token, whatever the token was?"

"When she goes to authenticate the provenance of the Lazarus parchment," Fred said slowly, "the scholars, curators, dealers, auctioneers, like to see the grandmother's letter itself. They prefer original documentation. The hotel people—what hold did the grandmother have to be able to trust them for god knows how many years?—they'll be happy with the Xerox copy. They've got the token, which is all they were expecting. Molly, I want you to go home now."

Fred had folded the letter into his shirt pocket, and begun to gather the rustling plastic wrappings into his arms.

"I can re-wrap them," Molly said. "I got pretty good at it. Mom never suspected. Shouldn't we leave things as we found them?"

"Your fingerprints are all over this plastic," Fred said. "Leave the matted drawings on the floor. The ones we didn't look into yet—leave them. Never mind. Don't touch anything else. Stand still. Let me think everywhere you've been in the studio. The rocker, yes…"

Fred carried the crackling wrappings to the cardboard box the artist had used for a trash can, next to his kitchen area.

"You're scaring me, Fred," Molly objected.

"I'm scared myself," Fred said. "I'm also perplexed. I've got to decide how to play this. Just stay still for two more minutes, then we'll get you on the road."

"Safe keeping in Warsaw?" Molly said. "He left it for safe-keeping in *Warsaw*?"

"Despite what was happening all around him, he was thinking of civilization as being on the side of humanity," Fred said. "An illusion many share. Safe as houses. He left the *Limbourg Bible* safe in Warsaw, along with the rest of the family. The bedridden grandfather, aunts, mother, wife, children, cousins, waiters, blind retired schoolteacher, pickpocket, sailor home on leave, hat maker, clarinet player...." Fred had grabbed up a brush rag from Jacob Geist's work area and, with it, was rubbing down everything Molly's fingers might have touched..."wastrel, libertine, wrestler, rickety child, three-year-old-girl with her stuffed bear. Hoping to save them all, to buy their safety, he left behind him what he held most dear, his Molly, his Terry, his Sam..."

"Don't, Fred. How about your prints?" Molly asked. "If you're trying to erase our presence..."

"There's too much of me here," Fred said. He'd come back to the stack of matted drawings they'd unwrapped and, using two rags, was rubbing the mats down and putting them back on the shelves. The Kordero stickers, adhering to the acetate wrappings, would go out with the trash.

Fred took the flashlight from Molly, wiped it, and said, "Ready?"

"You're sure you don't want us to look into those last ones?" Molly said.

"No. We'll talk outside. Before you step into the corridor, let me make sure the coast is clear."

"Who's Isabel?" Molly demanded. "You know. Fred, what are you thinking?"

"Right now, the only thing on my mind is, if you get caught in this, I won't forgive myself."

———

"It's as if nobody cares," Molly whispered as they went together along the dim corridor and down the stairs to the exit next to the loading dock. "The man died five days ago, five miles from here. His name's all over the Internet. He's a known quantity in the art world, a major talent—for heaven's sake, a fellow human being who has died in circumstances that themselves are worth a story—and nobody takes any notice. It's as if the poor man never existed. This great big dead place—it's like the way they teach history in the children's school. An empty hall where the voices of women bickering and children playing have been squashed out, and you only hear the bluster of a few men who happen to be born with a horse between their legs.

"Fred, what do you know about Isabel?"

They'd reached the outside door. Fred looked across the fenced parking area, which was lit by the refracted light from the street and from the Navy Yard.

"Go to your car and drive three blocks north," Fred directed, pointing. "I'm going back for that box. I'll join you."

"Should I be afraid?" Molly asked.

"Waste of energy," Fred assured her. "See you in five minutes. Hurry, now; so you're not seen with me."

Fred watched her until she reached Arnold Street, then ran upstairs again to get that box. Its contents must be destroyed. Otherwise Molly was linked to this building.

"Beamer, stay put," Fred whispered as he carried the box down with him. He locked the building, checked the street, and carried the box to his car.

Molly, in the shadow of the bridge, had parked with her lights off. The normal street business of a Tuesday evening— all that movement that never finds a place in history— continued: people driving home from work, or walking toward their night jobs, or a mistaken taxi trying frantically to find a rush-hour shortcut to Logan, while the angry businessman (born, maybe, with a taxi between his legs— but in this case the wrong driver) shouted in desperate frustration.

"OK," Fred said, sliding in next to Molly. "Next thing. I want to be with you when you do that test. I'm going to drop this box off at the Royal Court Hotel. The night man's a pal. He'll FedEx it for me to another pal, who'll burn it. I'm asking for trouble if I put it in a dumpster. And I don't want you accidentally tied to Chestnut Street either. I can't burn it there."

"Fred, we haven't done anything," Molly protested. "You haven't done anything."

"I don't like loose ends," Fred said. "People find a loose end, they pull it until they find someone to torment. This thing is as rippling with loose ends as a jelly fish. One person dies, there's a thousand stories cut off that can never be told again, and never finished." He tapped the pocket where he'd put the letter.

"Isabel's grandmother," Molly said. "That hotel will be able to give us her story, also her name. I'll get on the phone, or fax them, or they'll have E-mail. That's what you're thinking, yes? That the next step is to talk to Isabel?"

"I'm thinking of *this* poor son of a bitch," Fred said, tapping his pocket. "Under Vichy law it was a crime to be a Jew in Moulins. If the grandmother hid him, she charged him something to do it. Or if not, whether she did or not, she had no right to keep the scrap of painted skin he'd smuggled out of Warsaw. Another of the world's free agents. Hoping to buy his family's safety, I was thinking. But who knows?

Maybe he was just leaving his family in the lurch. People think being a victim means a person's virtuous. But we'll say, since we have to make it up, and all the evidence is ashes, that he planned to smuggle the rest of the *Limbourg Bible* out of Warsaw with his people.

"Let's rent a room and do that test. How about we do it in style at the Royal Court? I'll tell my pal we want the room for a quickie."

"Fred, you haven't told me what else you have to do in that building. But I can see it shouldn't wait. Another day or two before I do the EPT won't kill me. If you want me to I'll wait until we're together."

"I really do," Fred said. "It's selfish of me to think of myself at all at such a time—but—Molly—and we never said we wanted to...."

"Please," Molly pleaded, her face filled with distress. "Please, please, give me that box. I'll take it by the Charles Hotel in Cambridge on my way home. The concierge there is my pal. She'll send it for me on their account. Write me the name and address of your other pal, the one it's going to."

"You sure? About all this?" Fred asked. Molly nodded. "And you should eat, shouldn't you? In case you're..."

Molly wept while Fred wrote his note. *Dear Si. Burn this for me, will you? Everything's good here. All best, Fred.* She continued weeping while he wrote Si's address in Kansas. Weeping, she smiled and drove away.

"I played that wrong," Fred said. It was windy under the bridge, and cold, and damp, and noisy; but otherwise not that bad a place to live. Fred trudged across the damaged grass at the roadside and sat on the ground, leaning against a bridge pylon and watching the cold fog move in from the dirty harbor.

He stared for a while, not thinking, or not thinking words. The mind will not stop working unless you do something drastic to the head.

"What is it in me that won't let me alone?" he asked after a long spell looking at the air. "Joy, or something like it, flames out, and I want to mumble an objection, like the fellow whose impending execution makes him feel for thirty seconds that he has some real importance: *Molly, I don't know of a child in this world where I'm the father.*"

Almost as if it were alive, the stanchion he leaned against carried the pulse of the cars and trucks passing above his head.

"A child of mine," Fred said. "Does Molly believe that would destroy her family? I don't understand her, but I know those tears were anger as much as worry, or grief, or—she's got to be hungry too. I know I am."

Chapter 35

Fred watched the Lovett Shoe building until Beamer came out at 11:37, in the company of the young man she had admitted at nine. She locked the door and the two of them together crossed the lot, passed through the gap in the chain link fence, and, in earnest and familiar conversation, walked along Arnold Street past Fred's car and kept on going until they turned a corner.

"Richard," Fred remembered. "That guy's too small to take my place throwing Beamer into the sky and catching her."

The letter from Isabel's grandmother he took out of his pocket. "*Keep this from your mother*," he quoted. Why was that? Because she married a man named Katz? Let's say an American serviceman, why not? Or because she ran away from home with a bastard child? Because she stole money from her parents? Abused the family pet? Refused to attend the college of her mother's choice? Took the side of the father against the mother in some question? Told the authorities, after the war—what authorities? And what did they care?— how the parents had used their position to cheat and betray their clients and to turn them over to the authorities during the war? Or did she betray her father to the Vichy police, or to the Gestapo, or the Milice, for harboring enemies of the state? Or was it she who, after the war, betrayed him as a collaborator?

"What do I know? What do I need to know? Every life gone is a million unfinished stories. Pretend there may be such a thing as altruism in this world. I don't believe it—but you could make a fair story in which the French woman showed mercy to the fugitive, without any thought of gain, and the fugitive, in gratitude—both of them in ignorance of the parchment's potential value—what could it be worth after all when weighed against a life…?"

Fred let the thought dwindle until it disappeared into the golden fog from the Navy Yard.

"Unless it's someone else using his passport," Fred tried. "But no. That's Jacob's writing everywhere. His writing, and his cast of mind."

He put the grandmother's letter under a brick next to his car before he crossed the street, jangling the artist's keys. "I don't want that found on me," he muttered. "OK, you tricky bastard. Let's see how you did it."

———

The place where he must start had been obvious for days. Fred took the stairs for the top floor, poking along the wad of keys for likely candidates. As soon as he passed Beamer's landing, he pulled on the latex gloves the Store 24 had been good enough to sell him.

"And all the prisoners went free," he said, trotting along the fifth floor corridor past the empty rooms whose doors had gone to make up the artist's storage racks. Behind the entry marked KATZ/MONCRIEFF FINE ART a barely audible announcer was telling of floods in Tennessee.

KEEP OUT. Fred read the sign on the door to the fifth floor bathroom. The second key he tried opened the padlock. He'd done that right. New padlock. New hasp. New screws. New sign on a square of paper bearing a Rives watermark. The door opened toward him, followed by an engulfing smell of iron, clover and sugar, from the dark room.

"It may not be pleasant," Fred reminded himself, searching with a gloved hand until he found the light chain, pulled it, and lit a spectacle that made him gulp and continue, "You got that right too."

A couple dozen or so more of the generic plastic tubs were stacked next to the toilets. The smell was honey. The close air of the room was drenched in it. As many as a hundred of the emptied buckets, stacked one inside another, drooling strands of sweetness, had been neatly stacked in columns that reached almost to the ceiling.

The maggot born to the hive would grow up in this cloying stink of wealth. What must the first gasp of wild sky be like for the winged bee?

"Honey will do it," Fred said. That huge vat, which he knew from Jacob's floor, as well as from the photographs of veiled swimmers on Beamer's floor, in this instance had been filled to the brim with honey. It made a viscous glare against the hanging light, as Fred's inquiring shadow swung across it. From underneath the surface stared eyes—two pairs of human eyes, each with a third eye neatly placed above it, in the center of the forehead.

The bodies were golden naked: one man, one woman, laid heads to feet. Their limbs, seeking independence now that the tyranny of the brain had been replaced by physics, had caused the arms and legs to sprawl somewhat, so that the corpses seemed to hover in a clumsy dance, still well below the surface. The speedy decomposition of their bowels had been anticipated, because even within this heavy, sterile bath, their fermenting guts should by now have produced enough gas to lift their former owners' bodies to the air, and so start trouble in the building. This their killer had understood and had, industriously, taken into account. The belly of each corpse had been slit open from groin to breastbone, and the innards spirited away.

"What you got in them honey buckets, Jake?" Fred asked, glancing across the room at a neat pile of capped tubs. "As if I didn't know.

"What did you do, put something in their tea first?"

He stared down at the honeyed corpses of the two caricatures of painters. Buddy Moncrieff, the male, he recognized from Beamer's description. His gray Uncle Sam goat beard, shoved into a flabby point by the honey's weight, hung slightly to his left. The hands were too large for their arms, in the way of some older men. The nose was regal, the chest hair gray and sparse, the nipples flat and hairless, the genitals skinny, unkempt, balding. The nails on the man's feet were deeply yellow and ragged. Moncrieff's right arm had gotten involved with Isabel Katz's right leg in such a way that it was slightly lifted and entwined by it, as though in a gesture of affection.

The woman Fred knew mostly because, who else could she be? She was, as Beamer had described her, short and stocky, and probably around sixty. It was hard to say. The alien golden aura cast upon her by the substance around her did not permit a judgment as to the color of her hair, except that it must be dark. Her features were severe, her chins more than one and fewer than four. The fat content of her large breasts had heaved them toward the surface. The belly may have been of good size, since each cut side of its pouch showed a wide grin of fat, as well as being loose enough to float into a scallop. Both of her knees had lifted. The legs were free of the tub's floor. The small pearl nails of her feet had been well cared for. The pistol's muzzle poked out from under the woman's left buttock.

"If there is mercy in this world," Fred said; "and there is not—the son of a bitch left his own prints on that gun. On the tubs of livers and kidneys and intestines embalmed in honey, if not inside the apartment where he shot them.

"He meant to come back and finish here, thinking he had time. God knows he cleaned out their studio. But he didn't quite finish in here. Something pressed him, maybe Asgar Jincks. More likely Geist could not wait to get his money."

Fred swept the room one last time with his eyes. He had touched nothing, nor would he be required to. What Geist had left in here would hold at least until it got hot, maybe even after that: or until someone came looking for the fifth floor tenants, for that overdue consignment of one-size-fits-all paintings due in the Chelsea mall. Or until the folks arrived with the wrecking ball and made a Warsaw of the building.

Fred locked the door and listened at the stairs before he started down. Finding no hint of resident life on the fourth floor, he nipped along to Felice Beamer's studio and pulled from its door the manila envelope marked FRED.

Thanks, Beamer, Frank, he wrote on a scrap of paper that he left where the envelope had been.

Beamer was the loose end that most bothered him. She'd want to cover her own tail, so she might stay quiet. She was a loose end, though. Jacob Geist would have known how to tie it up. There was still room in the vat upstairs. But for Fred it was simply a problem that must remain a problem. He'd been around this building far too much, and with no good reason unless he told everything. And that he would not do. If he was lucky she'd remember him as Frank, and remember also that he knew about the hot plate.

On his way downstairs he looked at the picture she had given him, a handsome eight by ten in black and white, herself in free fall. "Free spirit," Fred said. She looked like a remarkably graceful frog fighting with cobweb.

He polished each key with the painting rag before he hung the ring on the molding next to Jacob's studio door. There was no point looking for more, or hanging around longer. What he would find elsewhere in the building, Fred already knew: the truck for hauling weight; the forklift, maybe; the drums that were intended, when he got to it, to hold, preserved in honey, heads, limbs, trunks; the bloody clothing waiting to be burned; the stacks of cash from Asgar Jincks's payment for first option on a page that did exist, which had been taken from a book that, in defiance of all probability, had managed to exist until the 1930s—but whose existence beyond that was no more likely than that of the many million souls deliberately pinched into oblivion by their fellow members in the tribe of *Homo sapiens.*

"May no one rest in peace," Fred swore, pulling the door of the Lovett Shoe building closed behind him.

Chapter 36

"It wasn't good, was it?" Molly said, when Fred came into the bedroom. She had lain down on top of the bed in her clothes, and had fallen asleep with the TV going. It was after two in the morning.

"No. Not good. I brought four sandwiches," Fred said. "Big choice tonight. Tuna, Italian, turkey, and ham-and-cheese. I'll be eating one in the kitchen if you care to join me."

"Don't eat the tuna," Molly said. "That's for me."

"I'm going to wake Sam and Terry," Fred said. "This life we lead: it has to be about something good."

Molly had tea made when Fred got downstairs. "Sam wouldn't wake up," he reported. "I suspect he hadn't been asleep much more than an hour. I turned his lamp off. Terry was glad to see me but she's not hungry for anything but cake. It'll be a small group. Which subs should I leave them?"

"They both complained about the Italian. I'd say that's the one for you."

Fred sat at the table freeing his sandwich from its windings. Molly was already up to her elbows in hers.

"You're not going to tell me, are you?" Molly asked. Fred waited until his first bite was washed down with tea. "No, is the quick answer. Also, should it ever come up, you were never in that building. You have children, and I may be caught. What you saw this evening on Chestnut Street, you never saw. You were not at Chestnut Street. I've explained that already to Teddy.

"The problem is, you can be compelled to answer questions about me, which you will not do. In response, they can jail you. Meanwhile, Sam and Terry need a mother."

"It's that bad," Molly guessed.

"It's hard to explain now. The next thing I'm going to do will make it harder," Fred said. He ate more of his sub, shook his head, then managed a smile. "Next subject," he said firmly. "That test. It's completely your business, and absolutely up to you, but when does the morning start? Does three a.m. constitute morning?"

"Oh, Fred, I'm so relieved and I'm so sorry," Molly said. "It turns out—once I got home—all of a sudden…"

Fred nodded. Molly dropped her sandwich and came around the table to put her arms around his head. "You may as well save the test," he said after a while. "In case you want it again."

They talked about this and that for a few minutes until Fred pried himself loose and told Molly, "That makes me a free agent, I guess. In about an hour I'm going to drive to Logan, start trying to make connections for Geneva. I have a telephone call to make first. You will not hear it, but it's your house and I can't help it if you *over*hear. Don't move. I'll call from the kitchen phone."

Hannah Bruckmann woke on the fourth ring. Fred said, "I will leave a message for you at the desk of the Cour Royal, Geneva. There's something you can help me sell. You know my voice?"

"Yes," Hannah said. "One idle question. Who does it belong to?"

"No one. Anyone who might have had a claim is dead. It's a story that's so sad it needs a million pages and it won't get even one. You can't give any provenance. By the time it's sold, it will belong to the United Nations fund for refugees, whatever they call it. I don't know what they call it."

"I know what they call it," Molly whispered.

"Or if it's easier I'll just sell it myself and give the proceeds to the fund. Who are the biggest and richest and cruelest bastards in this field, Hannah, you know and I don't," Fred said. "All I know how to do is be the cruel bastard standing beside you while you sell it for as much as it will bring. That single page is all that's left. How much commission do you want?"

"Fifty thousand and expenses," Hannah said quickly.

When he'd hung up Fred said, "All I can think to do is to subvert that goddamned thing till I can make it save a life or two. "

"You want me to give Clay a message?" Molly said.

"I'll call him from the airport. He'll be miffed, but he has a human streak and once he understands he won't dispute what I'm doing. Neither will Hannah. If she'd said she wanted less, though, I wouldn't trust her to make the sale," Fred said. "Five per cent of its value—she told me she might even get more for it—isn't much. Anything less, I'd figure she was dealing on the side."

"So, you'll be at the Royal Court, Geneva," Molly said.

"Hell no. Those places make me itch. I'll locate a starless hotel near the train station and—maybe I'll call you every night? Unless things here develop in a way that means we must break off contact for a while, until I make that sale. What do you say. Every night at about your ten o'clock? Take care of each other, will you, while I'm gone? You and Sam and Terry?"

"You want to shower or change or nap for an hour before you drive into the wilderness?"

"Thought I'd sit on your back steps and look at the yard," Fred said. "Once I get on a plane they'll let me kind of sleep on that."

"I'll sit with you," Molly said.

"It's cold."

"I'll find us a blanket."

About the Author

Nicholas Kilmer, born (1941) in Virginia, lives in Cambridge, Massachusetts and Normandy, France. A teacher for many years, and finally Dean of the Swain School of Design in New Bedford, Massachusetts, he now makes his living as a painter and art dealer. In 1964 he married Julia Norris, and with her has four children.

To receive a free catalog of other Poisoned Pen Press titles, please contact us in one of the following ways:

Phone: 1-800-421-3976
Facsimile: 1-480-949-1707
Email: info@poisonedpenpress.com
Website: www.poisonedpenpress.com

Poisoned Pen Press
6962 E. First Ave. Ste. 103
Scottsdale, AZ 85251